He didn't dare speak the truth . . .

"Why was a man with a gun heading for my room?" Samantha asked him again.

Chase continued his evasion. "Maybe he didn't like your hair or your clothes. Who knows what sets a lunatic off?" He could barely meet her eyes.

"You're telling me you think it's happenstance that a gunman would come after me?" Doubt filled her voice and fear her face.

Against his better judgment, Chase stepped inside the door and gathered her in his arms. "I'm not going to let anything happen to you," he said, fighting his desires. "Trust me."

How much longer could he maintain this charade? How much longer could he resist her?

And how much longer could he get her to trust him?

ABOUT THE AUTHOR

Kelsey Roberts lives in a small community outside Annapolis, Maryland, with her college-professor husband, Bob, and her eight-year-old son, Kyle. She paid close attention to the work-ethic lecture for, in addition to writing, she works full-time as a paralegal, owns a custom matting and framing business with her sister, and is in the process of devising a series of writing seminars. In her spare time, she enjoys traveling with her husband. In *Stolen Memories*, you may find hero Chase Lawson familiar—he's the brother of Cody, the hero from Kelsey's first book, *LEGAL TENDER*.

Books by Kelsey Roberts

HARLEQUIN INTRIGUE
248—LEGAL TENDER

Stolen Memories
Kelsey Roberts

Harlequin Books

TORONTO • NEW YORK • LONDON
AMSTERDAM • PARIS • SYDNEY • HAMBURG
STOCKHOLM • ATHENS • TOKYO • MILAN
MADRID • WARSAW • BUDAPEST • AUCKLAND

For Renae, Mika, Mary, Laura, Ellen, Melanie,
Linda and the other ladies who have filtered in
and out of our critique sessions. Without your
support and my overdraft protection, this would
never have become a reality.

ISBN 0-373-22276-9

STOLEN MEMORIES

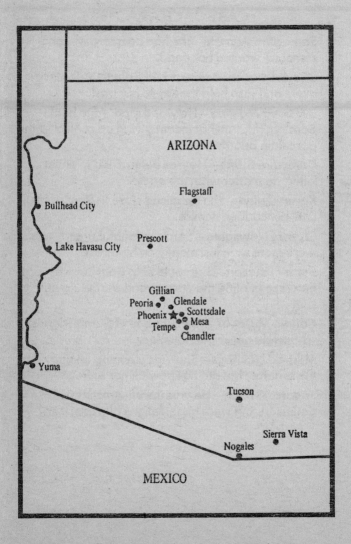

ARIZONA

Flagstaff

Bullhead City

Prescott

Lake Havasu City

Gillian
Peoria • Glendale
Phoenix ☆ • Scottsdale
Tempe • Mesa
Chandler

Yuma

Tucson

Sierra Vista

Nogales

MEXICO

CAST OF CHARACTERS

Samantha Parrish—She had no memory—and someone wanted her dead.

Chase Lawson—He watched Samantha's every move and also held the key to her past.

Dr. Greg Masters—He was supposed to heal Sam's mind, but that meant giving up control of the porcelain beauty.

Detective Burns—He was determined to catch a killer, no matter what the price.

Karen Quinn—She remained close to Sam right up until her sudden demise.

Charlie Newsome—Sam's unfaithful agent, was there more than just money on his mind?

Bunny Lawson—She could help Sam but was torn between healing the woman and shattering her son.

Connie Motegas—She was one of Sam's friends who might never get any older.

Mildred Hastings—She was planning on marrying the senator, but did he know all her secrets?

Senator Gillian—He was the all-American politician, but were his intentions all-American?

Prologue

He stood behind the safety of a thick tree trunk. His clothes were as black as the starless night sky. She was less than a hundred yards from him. Obviously, the ruse had worked.

He'd caught glimpses of her face in the glow of the streetlights as she'd passed beneath them. He liked her body and spent a few seconds fantasizing about what he might do to her. Although he was tempted, he knew his employer would frown on any deviation from the plan. He was being paid too well to risk disappointing his employer. Especially since there was another contract in the works.

Shaking his head to clear his thoughts, he silently resigned himself to the fact that he was here to do a job—period. She was less than fifty yards away now. He could hear the faint slap of her sneakers on the pavement.

"Damn!" he cursed softly as a jogger came into view just as he'd been about to make a move. "What kind of nut jogs in Central Park in the middle of the night?'' he grumbled as he moved out of his hiding place when the jogger was no longer a threat.

She was close enough now so that he could see the small, rectangular object clutched tightly in her hand. Her other hand protectively held the strap of her shoulder bag. It made him smile.

He caught the pleasant scent of her perfume just seconds before swinging the two-by-four. She crumpled to the ground, dropping the diary and her handbag in the process. He thought he might have heard the jingling of keys, but it was too dark for him to be sure.

''Thank you,'' he said as he grabbed the diary and stuffed it under his sweatshirt. ''And thank you again,'' he said as he snatched her purse. Straddling her body, he lifted his deadly weapon high above his head. ''How about a few more for good measure?'' he said with pure menace in his voice. ''My employer will be doubly pleased when I—''

''Hey!''

He looked up to see the jogger moving toward him.

''Sorry, Sam, ol' girl. Gotta go!'' As he ran through the woods, he could hear the jogger's frantic screams for help. He knew she was beyond help, though. Patting the concealed items, the man emerged from the woods and got into the rental car supplied as part of the contract.

Removing the diary and the purse, he carefully placed them in the glove box. Next, he removed the soiled black clothing and shoes and placed them in a pile on the floorboard, replacing them with the fresh items from the back seat. He started the car and headed for New Jersey, tossing the bits and pieces of his bloodstained clothing out the window at various points along the turnpike.

Chapter One

He stared out at the woman in the courtyard a half story below the window. She looked completely different. Gone were the golden tendrils of hair he'd watched dozens of men run their fingers through over the years. Of course, it had been part of her job, he reminded himself. She's an actress. The sultry looks and sensual kisses meant nothing.

"Then why is my gut all tied in knots?"

"What did you say?"

Chase Lawson turned, shrugging off his embarrassment at having spoken his thoughts aloud. "Nothing, Detective," he said to the pudgy man.

Detective Burns was watching him, a frown curving the corners of his lips downward.

Greg Masters, M.D., leaned back in his chair, his face an odd mixture of apprehension and defiance.

"Has Miss Parrish remembered anything?" Burns asked.

Dr. Masters shook his head as he answered, "No, I'm afraid her condition hasn't changed."

"That's too bad."

"She's definitely decided to leave the sanatorium, thanks to that damn invitation to attend her high school reunion," Dr. Masters added.

Chase couldn't help but smile behind his hand. Apparently, Samantha Parrish had developed a mind of her own after a year in this ritzy nuthouse.

"I'm worried about her safety, as well as about what could happen if she goes to Arizona." Dr. Masters reached up to massage the back of his neck.

"I see." There was no hint of concern in the detective's tone. "Have you told her about the note?"

"No," the doctor answered on a rush of breath. "I'm of the opinion that telling her would only add to her level of anxiety. Now, however, I suppose I won't have any choice."

"What about the incident on Route 17? Have you made any progress?" Burns asked the doctor.

When Dr. Masters shook his head, Chase felt this was his opportunity to reiterate his lingering reservations. "I still think you'd have better luck if you approached her about this straight on."

Both men looked at him, their faces bunched in near-mirroring frowns.

"We've been over this, Mr. Lawson," Dr. Masters stated.

"He's right, Chase," Burns agreed. "If we do anything to enhance her memory, we can't use anything she tells us as evidence. You know that."

"I think your plan's going to backfire," Chase predicted as he toyed with the brim of his hat.

"That's why you're here," Dr. Masters said.

Chase sighed, still not convinced that they were going about this the right way. Maybe there isn't a right way, he silently acknowledged. His hands balled into fists at either side of his body, and he had no choice but to play the hand he'd been dealt.

IT HAD BEEN three days since she had issued her ultimatum—free her, or else. Samantha allowed the uniformed host to escort her through the posh dining room. Greenhaven Sanatorium was famous for more than just its aggressive therapies. It was touted as *the* place where the rich and famous could recover from any number of maladies, while surrounded by all the comforts of home.

"Miss Quinn will be joining me for lunch," she told the dutiful attendant, who nodded before scuttling off. Sam was in the process of lowering herself into a chair when she felt his stare. The skin at the nape of her neck began to tingle, which in turn caused her stomach to tighten uncomfortably. Her fingers wrapped around the arms of the chair as she slowly raised her eyes to meet his.

That's when it happened. Briefly, suddenly and powerfully. Sam experienced a surge of recognition her injured brain was not yet able to comprehend. The feeling came and went in less than a second. Taking the menu and lifting it in front of her face, she swallowed and hid behind it long enough for the remnants of the uncomfortable feeling to abate.

Slowly, she lowered the menu, and peeked at the handsome stranger. He was big, not just tall, but huge! He looked completely out of place in the dainty floral surroundings done in soothing shades of pastel. The decor only served to heighten the contrast of his brooding darkness. He had no companion at the small table, only his Stetson occupied the seat to his left. But the remains of two extra plates indicated that he had not dined alone.

He was staring openly, with blatant interest apparent in his expression. His table was no more than ten feet away from her, and he watched her even after it was obvious that Sam had discovered his scrutiny. He'd inclined his head to one side, allowing ribbons of midday sun to highlight bluish streaks in his ebony hair.

"Do I know him?" she whispered to the print on the menu. Of course, going over to his table could turn into a disaster. What if his interest was nothing more than the curiosity of a former fan?

Sam grappled with her options for nearly a minute. Mentally, she played out a confrontation. "Excuse me, but I noticed you staring at me. Have we met before?" Sam groaned audibly. It sounds like some kind of desperate pickup line from a B movie.

"Hi!"

Slightly flustered, Sam's head turned toward the familiar voice.

Karen Quinn fell into the chair next to hers, depositing a sizable handbag on the floor with a thud.

"Hi," Sam returned, leaning close to her friend. "See that man over there? The one staring at me?"

Karen's eyebrows wrinkled, but she immediately began scanning the room. "Nope."

"What?" Sam yanked the menu down into her lap and found herself looking at an empty table. He was gone. "I'm losing my grip," she grumbled.

Karen reached out and patted the back of her friend's hand. "Mind telling me what's going on? I feel like I've walked into a play in the middle of Act Two."

Sam smiled. "There was this guy sitting there when I came in. He was staring at me, and I had another one of those flash things."

Karen's face became a mixture of distress and excitement. "You think you know him?" Karen sat up straight in her chair, a look of deep concern shrouding her green eyes. "Have you remembered something?"

Sam's shoulders slumped forward, making her appear even smaller than her petite five-foot frame. "No. It isn't like remembering. It's more of a feeling. I don't know how to describe it."

"Do you know who he was?"

"I don't have a clue," Sam acknowledged. After a deep breath and a short pause, she responded "I'm sure it was just my mind playing tricks on me again." Dismissing her thoughts of the handsome stranger, Sam said, "It's great to see you. Thanks for coming all the way out here just for lunch."

"Are you kidding me?" Karen scoffed. "The food here is so incredible, I think I've gained ten pounds just thinking about it!"

A polite, polished waiter arrived to take their order. Like everything else at Greenhaven, the server was attentive and accommodating. Although in her many months of captivity, Sam had come to resent having her every wish attended to.

"How are you feeling today?" Karen asked.

Sam inclined her head slightly and smiled at her visitor. Karen had been one of the few constants in her life these past few months. As Sam understood it, they had been little more than professional acquaintances prior to the attack. Karen had surprised Sam with her loyal friendship, especially when Sam compared it to that of other people who were supposedly very good friends of hers.

"How do I look?" Sam countered cautiously. Her memory might have been erased, but her vanity remained. It was nearly three months after the attack before she had dared to shed the brightly colored scarves she'd used to camouflage her baldness. The trauma surgeons had shaved her head in order to treat her injuries. It had taken weeks before the pale blond stubble began to grow, and then it had done nothing but stand straight on end.

"Great," Karen responded with a pout. "I can't believe your hair. I mean, I envied it when it was down to your waist, but I think I like it better short. It makes you look impulsive."

"Impulsive?" Sam repeated, touching the feathery ends of her bangs, which covered the faint scars near her hairline.

She watched as Karen ran her finger around the edge of the crystal water goblet. Her companion was sometimes given to these moments of introspection.

With one elbow on the table, Karen rested her heart-shaped face against her palm. "You were never an impulsive person."

There it was again, that stab of frustration that pierced Sam's composure every time she realized other people knew her better than she knew herself. "Really?" Sam queried.

"Heck, no! You were rigid as hell. You lived by lists and calendars. I used to think you couldn't catch a cold unless it was in your week-at-a-glance."

Sam laughed and gave Karen's reddish braid a tug. "I can't tell you the good it does me to have you come for a visit."

"You might not think so when I tell you why I'm here." Karen's expression grew solemn. Her eyes remained downcast long after the statement.

"Try me."

Recrossing her legs, Karen folded her hands in her lap. "I know you've said you weren't going back to *Secret Splendor.*"

"I can't see myself pretending to be someone else when I still don't have any idea who I am—or was," Sam answered jovially.

"Charlie's arranged for me to continue as your replacement," Karen blurted out in one breath.

Sam took in the upturned face that was wrinkled with worry, and she began to laugh. Karen looked positively stricken as she tried to remain poised.

"Is that all?" Sam asked with a dismissive wave of her hand.

"All! I couldn't sleep a wink last night wondering how you'd feel about my taking your place permanently. I mean, Carly was your role. You made her one of the hottest characters on daytime TV."

"That part of my life is over," Sam said simply. "I think it's a wonderful opportunity for you, and I hope you win an Emmy. I'll keep my fingers crossed."

Karen leaped from her seat and came over to Sam. The hug almost knocked the breath from Sam's body, as well as nearly toppling the chair.

"Charlie is lobbying hard to get them to expand the part. I'm hoping they'll give Carly a more important story line."

Sam marveled at the woman's enthusiasm and wondered, briefly, if she had ever exhibited similar excitement. "I think that's terrific."

"I can't thank you enough for personally contacting the producer when I told you I wanted the part. And signing with your agent has been a great boon to my floundering career, as well. He's done more for me in the past year than my last agent did in five." Although Karen's tone was enthusiastic, Sam noted a certain guarded expression in her eyes. It was probably nothing more than the last vestiges of discomfiture. Sam knew it was hard on people to be around her. At least Karen had stuck it out.

Charlie Newsome was just one of many of Sam's New York friends who found her difficult to be with since the attack. Most of her friends had come to visit in the beginning, then, as it became apparent that her memory wasn't going to return immediately, they had gradually faded from her life. Sam didn't begrudge them their lack of interest, but she did resent what they took with them. They were her link to the past, and with each departure, Sam lost access to those parts of her personality erased or hidden away somewhere in her mind.

The extent of Charlie's caring had been two visits—then nothing. Obviously, his interest in her hinged on a fifteen-percent cut.

"I'm really happy for you, Karen. I think you'll do great as Carly. And it'll be nice to have them write her out of that silly kidnapping story line. What were the writers thinking of? Who do they think would believe that drivel?"

Karen laughed, but the flash in her green eyes appeared clouded. "They had to come up with something quickly after your..."

"Attack," Sam said firmly. "It's okay. We can say the 'A' word."

"You know," Karen said hesitantly, her eyes fixed on a point in the distance. "I've never understood what happened that night."

"Don't ask me," Sam teased.

"It was totally out of character for you. Sam, have you remembered anything? Anything that might explain what you were doing in Central Park at two in the morning?"

Shaking her head, she sighed. "No, and the doctors say I'll probably never remember that part." In response to Karen's troubled expression, Sam continued, "Something about the mind shielding the consciousness from horrors. They believe my mind will protect me from ever remembering anything connected to the attack. Besides, the incident itself is probably permanently erased. Organic in origin." The last bit of information was spoken in a perfect impersonation of Dr. Masters's annoyingly emotionless intonation.

"Maybe that's for the best," Karen said quickly. "I guess that means you won't be able to help the police with their investigation?"

"I have this strange feeling that Detective Burns knows more about what happened that night than I do."

Karen's head whipped around, and her eyes fixed on Sam. "Why do you say that?"

Sam shrugged. "No reason, just a feeling."

"Has he said something that makes you think the police have a lead?" Karen pressed.

"No, nothing like that." Sam scraped the last bit of sinfully rich chocolate mousse out of a silver bowl with her spoon. She appreciated her friend's apparent concern, but she didn't feel like rehashing old news. "Let's talk about something else, okay?"

"I didn't mean to upset you," Karen said, wearing that stricken look again.

"Not you, too!" Sam groaned. "I can't stand that reaction."

"What reaction?"

"The pitiful one!" Sam said emphatically. "I'm not a fragile piece of china, Karen. I'm so sick of people treading on eggshells whenever they open their mouths around me that I could just spit! I wasn't crazy when they put me in this place, but if I stay here much longer, I'm not sure if I'll leave here sane."

"Geez, I'm sorry," Karen whispered. "I didn't mean anything. Really."

Sighing, Sam's expression softened and she smiled. "No, I'm the one that should be sorry. I guess I'm a bit tense about leaving."

"You don't have to leave here, Sam. In fact, you shouldn't leave until you feel you're ready. I think you're making a mistake."

"I know," Sam said as she patted the top of Karen's hand. "And I know you mean well, but I'm ready," she assured her friend. "I'm just a little afraid of striking out on my own. Leaving Greenhaven is like leaving home for the first time. I'm excited, but at the same time I'm . . . apprehensive."

Karen's mouth twitched at the corners. Sam appreciated her friend's forced, but supportive, smile. "I'm no doctor, but that sounds like pretty rational thinking to me."

"Dr. Masters doesn't think so. He believes I'm setting myself up for disaster."

"He has a point, Sam," Karen said. "There's no telling what might happen when you're out there on your own. What if you get your memory back and can't handle it?"

"Don't be silly," Sam insisted. "Nothing's going to happen to me. Frankly, I'd love to get my memory back. As it is, I only know what other people have chosen to tell me. I feel like everyone knows more than I do. It's infuriating!"

"Enough with the maudlin thoughts!" Karen said firmly and pushed herself away from the table. "Let's go outside and take a walk. The exercise will do me good after the trillion calories I just consumed."

SAM WAS STILL SMILING from her visit with Karen as she made her way back to her room alone.

"Miss Parrish?"

Sam stopped and turned her head in the direction of the nurse's station. "Yes?"

"You have a visitor. He's waiting for you in the lounge."

Sam was about to question the woman further, when the buzz of the intercom sent the nurse scurrying in the opposite direction. With a shrug, Sam ventured the twenty or so steps to the area enclosed in floor-to-ceiling glass. It had been designed to have the look and feel of a bright living room; but Sam always felt as if she were an insect under glass whenever she was forced to visit the lounge.

It was *him!* She was sure of it, even though he was standing with his back to her. His worn Stetson dangled from the long, squared fingers of one hand. The shirt encasing his massive shoulders appeared stiff and freshly laundered, and was a stark contrast to the soft, faded denim jeans belted around his tapered hips. He shifted his mass from one booted foot to the other. The movement pulled the fabric taut against powerfully built thighs.

Maybe what she'd experienced earlier in the dining room was more than just a feeling—maybe it was instinct. And perhaps something about this man would trigger a memory.

"I'm Samantha Parrish," she announced with just a twinge of excitement in her voice.

He turned then, his face a hard mask of unreadable emotion. Sam found the intensity of his dark eyes unnerving; they were very nearly as black as his hair. The set of his jaw surprised her almost as much as the way his eyes roamed over her as if she were a mannequin in a store-window display.

"Chase Lawson," he said with a deep voice that held just the hint of a Western drawl. His eyes moved up and fixed on her face. Sam had the distinct impression he was waiting for something.

After what seemed like an interminable period of time, it became obvious to her that he was glued to the spot. Sam crossed the room so that she stood only a few feet from him. The sun's rays streamed in the glass behind him, outlining the dark man in a rich, golden aura. A faint scent, a mixture of soap and subtle cologne, filled her senses as she studied his sharply angled features.

Finally, he smiled. It was warm and brilliant and more affecting than the sun behind him.

"I guess you weren't expecting me."

Her eyebrows wrinkled as she stared at the man before her. "I'm afraid you have me at a disadvantage. And no, no one said anything about *you* to me." *She'd have remembered if one of the staff had mentioned a man as gorgeous as the one standing in front of her!* Blinking hard, Sam pushed those thoughts from her head. "Are you a doctor, Mr. Lawson?"

He laughed, a deep, rich sound that seemed to reach out and caress her ears. Every cell in her body responded to the warmth of his laughter. *What's wrong with me? The first attractive man I encounter in months, and I turn into a pile of raging hormones!*

Misinterpreting her reaction as censure, he checked his laughter, though a twinkle of humor still lingered in his eyes. "I'm not a doctor."

"Okay," she told him as she tossed back her head in order to meet those dark arresting eyes head-on. "Then why are you here to see me?"

A bronze hand went up to adjust the collar of his shirt. He swallowed before beginning an explanation. "I assumed Dr. Masters had already covered all this with you."

She was totally confused and about to say as much, when the good doctor, flanked by Detective Burns, appeared in the doorway.

"I thought I told you to wait in my reception area." Dr. Masters shot the larger man a wilting look, but it didn't appear to faze Chase in the least. The doctor came to her side, placed his arm around her shoulder, and using the same condescending tone, he spoke to her softly. "Samantha, I think it would be better if we continued this in my office."

"Fine." She shrugged away from him, annoyed. "Would someone mind telling me what 'this' is?"

"All in good time," the doctor promised, placing his hand at her elbow and steering her out of the room.

As they navigated the maze of corridors, Sam was acutely aware of the man walking behind her. While the four of them moved in silence, Sam used the time to try to piece Chase Lawson into the puzzle of her life. Was he somehow connected to her past? If so, why hadn't she come across his name before? It was obvious from his coloring and the high definition of his cheekbones that he was a Native American. It seemed improbable that she would forget a man as gorgeous as him.

Dr. Masters ushered them into his office and assigned seats. Sam found herself sandwiched between the detective and Chase. Out of the corner of her eye, Sam noted how utterly relaxed Chase appeared. One large hand cradled the brim of the Stetson, the other draped casually over the armrest. One leg was crossed over the other, displaying a large portion of a snakeskin boot beneath his pant leg.

The scent was there, too. Fresh, outdoorsy and utterly masculine. Sam wondered, yet again, if this sudden attack of feminine interest was a result of her months of confinement or if it was a reaction to this man in particular. At any rate, she liked anything that broke up the monotony of her days at Greenhaven. And Chase was definitely a welcome break from the seemingly unending stream of police personnel, psychologists and physical therapists.

Dr. Masters began speaking, which prevented her from further exploring her reaction to the man seated next to her.

"I took the liberty of contacting Detective Burns a few days ago, after you informed me of your plans to leave Greenhaven." The doctor didn't even attempt to conceal his fervent opposition to her decision to leave.

First Karen, now Masters! She was sick of people treating her as if she were incapable of functioning outside the hedged lawns of the sanatorium. Suppressed indignation pulled her mouth into a thin line, and she leveled her eyes on the doctor. Bracing herself against the back of the smooth leather chair, she stemmed the flow of frustration churning in her stomach.

"I don't know why you took it upon yourself to do such a thing," she said tightly. "I'm certain Detective Burns has more important things to do than concentrate on my agenda." And what, she wondered silently, did the broad-shouldered Mr. Lawson have to do with any of this?

"Not true," Burns inserted. His pronounced New York accent slurred the words into an unbroken stream of chopped syllables.

Angling herself slightly, Sam shifted her attention to the detective. "And why is that?"

Steepling his fingertips, Burns tapped the pads of his pudgy forefingers against the lower of his two chins. "Your case is still open, which means your whereabouts remain my concern."

"Come on, Detective. It's been over a year since the mugging."

Burns visibly stiffened inside his rumpled suit. One hand went up to arrange the thinning strands of hair, and a frown produced deep crevasses in his full, round face. Sam found his expression fell short of intimidating. "I can assure you, we're still handling your case as a priority," the detective intoned.

She supposed she should feel some semblance of gratitude, but it just wasn't there. Letting out a breath, she lowered her eyes and stared at the pale, rose-colored polish on her nails. "I know how much time you've put into your investigation, Detective, but I think it's time we threw in the towel, don't you?"

"Not yet," Burns responded quickly. So quickly that Sam couldn't help but wonder why he was so determined to keep going, when the investigation had never really gotten very far off the ground in the first place.

"Please continue with the case, then. It's your time to waste as you see fit," she told him. "And if you need anything, I'll be sure to leave a number where I can be reached in Gillian, Arizona."

"I'm afraid it isn't quite that simple."

Sam's head shot up and she met the detective's eyes. "What isn't that simple?"

"You're a material witness to a felony, Miss Parrish. Your cooperation is necessary to the investigation."

"Cooperation?" she repeated in a high-pitched voice of disbelief.

Burns made a production out of adjusting his tie. "When we have a suspect, we'll need you. There are several procedural matters that require quick action once we make an arrest."

"Arrest who? In case you've forgotten, Detective, I can't remember anything about that night. Hell, I can't remember anything about *me!*" Scrambling to her feet, Sam could feel her heart pounding against her rib cage. She looked to Dr. Masters, but sensing no ally there, she turned to Chase.

The compassion brimming in his dark eyes caught her off guard. Why was a total stranger looking at her as if he understood?

"Calm down, Samantha," Dr. Masters directed in that even, paternal tone that was about as soothing as walking on broken glass.

She wanted to scream but the months of therapy had conditioned her reaction. Like Pavlov's dog, her practiced response was to take slow, deep breaths until her heart no longer beat erratically.

"I *am* calm," she insisted between clenched teeth. "I just don't understand this. All I want to do is get on with my life. There's no reason for me to stay here. And who knows? Going back to Arizona and attending my high school reunion might help me get my memory back."

Sam looked in turn at the three pairs of eyes. Burns appeared to be annoyed by her tirade. The doctor's eyes reflected concern with just a touch of impatience. But Chase Lawson's eyes sparkled with amusement. His dark head inclined fractionally, silently conveying his approval. She swallowed, alternately thrilled and perplexed by his reaction.

"No one here is telling you not to go," Dr. Masters said. "We just want to set some ground rules."

Forgetting her dark, silent ally for a moment, Sam glared at her physician. "What do you mean, ground rules? You're my doctor, not my keeper."

"You're exhibiting a great deal of hostility, Samantha."

"Maybe that's because I feel a bit hostile."

"Miss Parrish." Burns rose to stand between the warring parties. "I think the good doctor may have misstated this situation."

"I didn't realize we had a situation," she said hotly.

Burns continued swiftly, "What we have is the potential for a real problem because of your sudden decision to leave here. I think we can strike a deal, but you'll have to hear me out first."

As much as she would have liked to tell him to stick his "deal" in his ear, Sam decided she would have nothing to lose by listening. Still, she remained standing. She wasn't quite ready to volunteer total acquiescence. Besides, she knew hearing the detective out was the only way she'd ever find out how Chase fit into the scenario.

Crossing her arms in front of her chest, Sam tilted her head to one side, indicating her willingness to listen.

Burns quickly began speaking when he realized he had her reluctant cooperation. "There are a few logistical problems to work out, but I think you'll still be able to head out west," Burns said.

He paused, obviously waiting for her to gush words of eternal thanks. Sam narrowed her eyes but said nothing.

"The way I see it, there are three problem areas with your going to Arizona," he said after a moment. "First, Dr. Masters tells me that on the slim chance that you get your memory back, it could spook you to the point where you'd crack." Dr. Masters interrupted the detective by coughing loudly. "I mean, the trauma of it could be a serious shock to your... emotional well-being," Burns amended.

Sam shook her head and nearly laughed at the brusque man struggling to recite psychological theory. "Go on," she prompted.

"Second, there's the fact that you are a material witness, and, technically, I can have you placed in protective custody until there's a resolution to the case."

"At the rate you're progressing, Detective, I could be in protective custody until I grow old and die."

Burns ignored her little dig and continued, "Which brings us to the third issue—your safety."

"Forgive me, Detective. But I'm going to go out on a limb here and venture a guess that Gillian, Arizona—population, three thousand—is just a tad safer than Manhattan."

"You don't get it, do you?" Burns asked loudly with a shake of his head.

Not expecting the flash of anger from the detective, Sam flinched at the harshness of his tone.

"No, I don't."

"When you leave here, the press will be all over you. The papers are bound to print where you're going and why. You're a celebrity, Miss Parrish. The public wants to know all about your recovery, just like they ate up all the details of your mugging and the resulting amnesia."

"Are you holding me responsible for what ends up in those trashy tabloids?"

"No," Burns answered quickly. He rubbed both hands over his ruddy face and said, "Lady, I'm just trying to give you a feel for what we're up against here. When the press gets wind of the fact that you're leaving the hospital, your face, as well as your itinerary, will be plastered in papers and on TVs all over the country. The grocery-store rags are the least of my worries."

"So, I'll have Charlie release some sort of statement," she countered easily.

"This isn't working," Burns said to Chase and Dr. Masters. "Do you know how people react to the word *amnesia*, Miss Parrish?"

"It's hard for people to believe," Sam answered without emotion.

Burns face spread into a broad, satisfied grin. "You're catching on. And how do you think the guy that attacked you is going to feel when he hears you're going off to Arizona, which may or may not trigger a return of your memory?"

Sam swallowed hard as fear inched its way along her spine. "Are you telling me that you think whoever attacked me will try again?"

"I'm just saying it's a possibility." The detective's voice softened. "Which is why I've asked Chase to help us out."

Her eyes moved to Chase, only to find his handsome features passive. He rose slowly to his full height, well above six feet. One hand still clutched the Stetson.

"What is he? Some sort of bodyguard?" Sam wailed. "Well, you can forget that right now! I can't get on with my life with some muscle-bound shadow following me everywhere. Thanks, but no thanks."

Woodenly, Sam strode toward the door. Her pretty face was frozen into a sculpture of open but controlled, fury. She refused to so much as look in the direction of that towering presence. Just as Sam reached for the doorknob, the stern, predictable sound of Dr. Masters's voice bit into her composure.

"I thought you might react this way," Dr. Masters said with the same glee as a child experiencing something wonderful for the first time.

Something in that calm, slightly haughty voice sent her over the edge. Furious, fists knotted by her sides, Sam turned and glared at the man on the opposite side of the desk.

"Yes, Doctor. I've no doubt your skill and training allowed you to anticipate my reaction. Well, anticipate this—I'm not going to spend the rest of my life in fear. And I'm definitely not going to have my every move monitored by some handpicked baby-sitter with bulging biceps. Having him around will only draw more attention to me. Attention I neither want nor need at this point in my life."

"I can assure you, Samantha, no one in Gillian will think a thing of seeing you and me together," Chase interjected softly.

She wasn't sure what disturbed her more, the sound of her name on Chase's lips, or the self-assurance with which he'd calmly dismissed her concern.

"Really? And how can you be so sure?"

Chase took several steps forward. He was close enough for Sam to feel the warmth of his breath against her face.

"I promise you, there won't be any problem with us being together in Gillian," he assured her in a quiet, almost seductive whisper. Peering down from his superior height, Chase's eyes met and held hers.

"That's what makes this arrangement so perfect," Burns announced excitedly.

Chase stood over her, casting an ominous shadow as he said, "You see, Sam, we were high school sweethearts."

Chapter Two

The impact of his revelation made her knees go weak. Her mouth gaped open. Involuntarily, one hand reached out blindly, grasping the solid muscle of Chase's forearm.

Sam's eyes frantically searched his face. She tried desperately to summon a memory of their high school days together. "You and I were..." Her faint voice trailed off.

"Yes," Chase answered quietly, his features softened to match his voice. "We've known each other for years—since we were kids."

"Mr. Lawson!" Dr. Masters rushed over, prying them apart by inserting himself between them. "I think we need to give Samantha a chance to absorb this information."

"No!" she protested.

"Now, now," Dr. Masters soothed. "There will be plenty of time for you and Mr. Lawson to catch up.

There's no need to rush things. We've talked about how unproductive your impatience can be.''

"Talking to the man is not impatience. Nor is it rushing things," Sam said scathingly. The initial shock of discovering his link to her past slowly gave way to an urgent need for details. "I want to talk to someone who knew me before I came to New York. Up until now, I've only been told bits and pieces about my life in Manhattan and virtually nothing about my childhood."

Reluctantly, Dr. Masters stepped aside, only to be replaced by the intrusive presence of Detective Burns. "I'm afraid your reunion will have to wait until tomorrow. Chase and I have some final details to attend to this afternoon."

"Surely that can wait!" Sam beseeched.

"I'm afraid not," he said. "Not if you want to go forward with your plan to leave the sanatorium tomorrow."

Burns was asking her to exercise extraordinary patience. In the end, after being assured that Chase would be waiting for her when she arrived at her Manhattan apartment, Sam reluctantly watched him leave with Burns.

"I wish you'd give yourself more time, Samantha," Dr. Masters said.

Sam walked over to the window behind the desk, her eyes fixed on the duo moving together through the parking lot. "I know," she answered. "Everybody thinks I should give it more time. Everybody but me, and that's what matters."

She turned to find her confession had produced a deep frown on the doctor's face. "What did you feel when you met Mr. Lawson?" Dr. Masters asked.

Swallowing, Sam tried to find an appropriate name for it. "It was the same as when you showed me the photo of my grandmother. A fragment of something, but I couldn't hold on to it." Dejected, Sam leaned against the windowsill and tried to concentrate.

"If that's true, then being around Lawson could possibly bring back at least part of your memory."

Sam's face brightened at the possibility.

Dr. Masters apparently regretted his statement. His head rocked from side to side, and the downturned corners of his mouth dampened her budding hopes. The chair squeaked as he shifted his weight. "Don't you think it would be best for you to go to your reunion and then return here? Where we can continue our work?"

Sam let out a breath and looked directly into the doctor's eyes. "Forgive me, Doctor. But our work consists mostly of your hand-feeding me scraps of my life and then asking me the same litany of questions. It hasn't worked yet, so I have no choice but to get on with my life."

"I still think you ought to stay in New York, where we can talk about things."

"And Karen thinks I ought to stay in New York. So does Detective Burns and Polly, the night nurse," Sam explained. "I know everyone is concerned about me, but I'm not sick anymore. I can walk and talk and function, and I just want the opportunity to do that without having to discuss my every action and feeling."

It was only by reminding herself that Dr. Masters had helped her cope during those early days that Sam was able to keep the frustration she felt from tainting her words with sarcasm. He had, after all, seen to it that she had gotten excellent care; including tutors and everything else that had enabled her to evolve into her present state as a functioning shell of a human being. Why, she silently wondered, couldn't he understand her need to become whole? Why couldn't any of them understand?

Knowing a debate on the subject would prove fruitless, Sam excused herself, feigning fatigue. She raced back to her suite, her heartbeat pounding in her ears with excitement. Could Chase Lawson be the key that would unlock her past? *Key*—the word brought on a sudden flash of inexplicable fear.

That night, a recurring dream kept her awake into the wee hours. It was really more of a nightmare—one she'd experienced often since the attack. She was walking toward the figure of a woman. The woman had her arms outstretched to Sam. In spite of the welcoming figure, there was something dark and evil in the dream. But whenever Sam turned to look at whatever evil lurked beyond the woman, she'd inevitably awaken, her body bathed in perspiration. Everyone, it seemed, had a theory about the dream. Sam didn't care about the theories; all she knew was that the dream chilled her to the core.

THE NEXT MORNING Sam dressed long before the first light of day spilled over the expertly landscaped grounds of Greenhaven. Carefully, knowing full well the press would be out in force, Sam dressed in beige silk pants and a bright red blouse.

She stood in front of the mirror, studying her reflection. She looked every inch the poised, polished celebrity. The simple elegance of her clothing projected just the right image she would need to shield herself from the speculation she was sure would follow her from the sanctity of the sanatorium.

The slacks were a bit loose, since she'd lost some weight during her recovery. At least she assumed as much after watching endless hours of videotape provided by her producer. The Samamtha Parrish she saw on the screen—star of the daytime drama *Secret Splendor*—was that of a total stranger. She had watched the tapes over and over, studying herself through the detachment of her amnesia. In a couple of scenes, she'd been locked in the arms of her co-star, simulating intimacy. For the life of her, Sam couldn't recall ever kissing anyone; yet there it was on screen. Recalling that scene, an image of herself locked in Chase Lawson's powerful arms now filled her mind. Was it a memory? she wondered.

She paced the room, waiting for the car that would take her to her apartment. Sam had been there once, as part of a mental-health field trip. The therapy had been designed to see if anything about the apartment seemed familiar. She'd been terrified that first time, still in a state of confusion over the erasure of her memory. Now, knowing Chase would be waiting there, she felt much less apprehensive. "There is something to be said for having a large man in your life," she told her reflection.

The drive seemed interminable, especially since Sam had no sense of the distance from Greenhaven to Manhattan. She'd asked the driver "how much longer" so many times that he'd raised the glass partition between the front and back seats. Her midafternoon arrival at the posh Manhattan high rise had created quite a mob scene. An unbroken line of manned cameras, some perched on tripods, edged the curb for the entire block across from her building. The lenses were poised and trained on the entrance.

"Stay put until I open the door for you," the driver instructed through a speaker as the sleek automobile cut a path through the assembled mob and came to an abrupt and jolting halt.

Obediently, Sam remained behind the safety of the darkly tinted glass. She braced herself for the flurry of questions and the blinding flash of cameras. The second the car door opened, her world was reduced to a frantic volley of strobe lights and a barrage of shouted inquiries.

Blinded by the flashbulbs, Sam felt herself being tugged from the seat. She was aware of nothing but the strength of the arm that locked itself around her waist, nearly lifting her out of the car and off the pavement. Her movement through the crowd was swift. It wasn't until the sounds of the voices became muffled that she realized she was safely inside the lobby.

Opening her eyes, Sam was stunned to discover her escort was none other than Chase Lawson. Peering up at him through the lingering red spots from the flash-bulbs, she offered him a grateful smile.

Guiding her toward the elevator, Chase poked the call button and absently stuffed the hem of his chambray shirt into the waistband of his jeans. It was only then that Sam realized her own blouse had been dislodged during the short trip from the car to the building. "They're animals!" she observed, though she couldn't keep the hint of amusement out of her voice. Animals or not, she was free. Sam slipped her handbag beneath one arm in order to straighten her clothing.

"I don't know how you put up with that stuff," Chase said, clearly annoyed.

"I don't, either," she joked. "But then again, I don't remember my own birthday."

The muscles in his broad shoulders stiffened. "Sorry, I didn't mean—"

"Hey." Sam reached out and tentatively placed her hand against his arm. She could feel the muscles beneath the fabric. They were tight and cordlike. "Let's get one thing straight from the outset... Don't apologize for making simple remarks that refer to memory. We'll never get along if you measure every word before it comes out of your mouth. Okay?"

She felt the muscles relax, and her eyes went up to search his face. His head dipped fractionally lower, his dark eyes regarding her carefully.

"Fair enough," he said just as the doors slid open.

They entered the small compartment, and Sam managed to sneak a quick look at his impressive shoulders before he turned to press the button that would take them to the penthouse apartment. Chase appeared to fix his attention on the progress of the doors sliding shut.

"April thirtieth," he said as the elevator jerked to life. In response to Sam's quizzical look, he added, "Your birthday."

Nodding, she lowered her eyes to the floor. "It was a whole lot easier to remember when I had that plastic bracelet on my wrist." Standing beside him, Sam was suddenly very aware of their closeness. Chase's sheer size dominated the small elevator. And whatever space wasn't consumed by his size was filled with the pleasant scent of his cologne. Sam breathed it in as if it were pure oxygen. Unexpectedly, she found herself experiencing a wave of disappointment when the doors slid open upon reaching the top floor.

They took two steps and Chase unlocked the door to her apartment, then stepped aside, allowing Sam to enter the starkly decorated rooms.

"This place looks like no one lives here," she said with a sigh. Tossing her purse on the chair closest to her, she placed her hands on her slender hips and eyed the furnishings. The walls, along with every stick of furniture, were white. Plain, unimaginative and sterile. She knew from her previous visit that the other rooms were decorated similarly, white with an occasional splash of red or blue.

"I don't know," Chase mused aloud. "It's not so bad."

"How can you say that?" she retorted. "It's about as homey as an operating room."

Chase grinned. "Well, it is rather stark compared to your grandmother's place."

"How so?" she asked, knowing it was as good a place to start as any. Prior to her horrible nightmare, she'd lain awake the night before thinking of hundreds of questions she wanted to ask him, and she was determined to start immediately.

"Mind if I put on a pot of coffee before we start the inquisition?" he teased.

Sam found herself blushing with embarrassment. "Sounds like a great idea, but let me do it."

Chase followed her into the narrow kitchen, nearly running her down when she came to an abrupt halt. The feel of his body against her back caused an involuntary gasp to escape from Sam's slightly parted lips.

His hands gripped her shoulders, steadying her. His fingers were long and there was an immediate warming of her skin in response to his touch. Awkwardly, she lurched forward, away from him.

"Sorry," they mumbled in unison.

"It was my fault," Sam insisted, though she refused to turn and face him until her pulse calmed to a manageable rate. Again her brain struggled with the question of her reaction to this man. Did some part of her remember him? That might explain her strong physical attraction and interest.

Sam forced a pleasant smile to her lips and began searching for the coffeepot. It was hard to ignore the fact that she felt like a stranger in her own home. She decided the best way to keep from thinking about it was to talk. "Tell me about my grandmother."

Chase looked completely relaxed as he leaned against the smooth edge of the countertop, arms folded across his massive chest. "Gran was a great lady. Who knows? Maybe going back tomorrow and surrounding yourself with her things will help jog your memory."

Suddenly, the realization that she was going to spend the night with this man hit her. It must have shown in her expression, because Chase's face was instantly etched with deep concern.

"If you've changed your mind about going home, just say the word."

"What? I mean, no, I haven't changed my mind about going . . . home." The word felt foreign on her tongue. "I feel like I've been frozen in time for the past year. I can't wait to try my hand at living a normal life in normal surroundings."

He nodded, but Sam thought she noticed a flicker of some feeling she could not identify cloud his eyes.

"I take it you liked my grandmother?" she asked as she made coffee.

"Yep," he answered with genuine affection in his tone. "She was one hell of a human being."

"Did she bake great cookies? What?" she asked dryly.

Chase laughed softly, causing his chest to rise and fall. The movement drew her attention to his physique.

"Gran didn't cook. She was too busy—always on the go. If it didn't go from the freezer to the oven to the table, your grandmother didn't serve it."

Sam found herself smiling with him. "Hardly the image I had. From the pictures I've seen, she looks like a kindly old lady. Since no one at Greenhaven knew her, I had only the photos to go on."

"She was a fine lady," Chase repeated. "She just wasn't what you might call the conventional grandmotherly type."

"Were she and I close?" Sam asked, her face turned up to his.

"Very. There was a lot of love there. I guess that's why every kid in Gillian naturally gravitated to your house. In a small, conservative town like Gillian,

Gran's was the place to hang out for most of the kids between the ages of thirteen to about twenty."

"I've gotten a lot of cards from various people in Gillian." *I don't recall receiving one from you,* she added silently as the shrill sound of the phone interrupted her train of thought. Chase reached for the receiver. He listened for a few seconds, then covered the mouthpiece with his hand.

"One of your neighbors called the cops about all the press," he explained. "The doorman wants you to know they're about to send them away."

"Fine with me," she said with a devilish smile.

"Do you want to talk to them first? They might say unflattering things about you if the cops send them packing before you've made an official appearance."

"I don't care," she said firmly. "I'm not particularly interested in what the press thinks of me."

Chase gave the appropriate instructions to the doorman. Sam felt a rush of something dance through her veins. She found she genuinely liked her newfound freedom, as well as her new companion.

Dangerous thoughts, she told herself, and forced her mind to think of the image Chase had given her of her grandmother. When she heard the last sputter of water drip from the coffeemaker, she absently moved to the third cabinet from the left and retrieved two mugs from the lowest shelf. She had just started pouring, when she discovered Chase staring at her.

"What?" she inquired.

His expression was one of total bewilderment. "How did you know where to find the mugs?"

Sam looked at the matching ceramic cups as if they were creatures from an alien world. "I don't know," she murmured. "It happens every now and then."

"Is that good? I mean, doesn't it mean you're remembering?"

Sam shrugged. "They tell me it might mean that, or it's just a fluke thing in my brain. No one seems to know."

"Does it happen often?"

Sam shook her head. "Nope. In fact, now I can't remember where I got them from just a second ago."

At Chase's confused expression, she explained, "I get these flashes, bits and pieces that don't usually stay with me. One day, about a month ago, I was chatting with one of the patients at Greenhaven when, out of the blue, I recommended a certain dry cleaner here in the city. Now I couldn't recall their name if my life depended on it. Some things just float in and out. I don't seem to have any control."

After absorbing her words, Chase dropped the subject, guided by the sudden apprehension apparent on her face. "Let's go into the living room, and I'll tell you some more about Gran."

"Excellent idea," Sam said. She followed him, glad to be embarking on a conversation that didn't begin with the phrase "How do you feel about..." Her eyes fixed on the breadth of his shoulders and the slight swagger in his walk. Sam didn't need her memory to realize the man had one heck of a sexy walk.

Purposefully, she took the seat opposite him in one of the puritanical white chairs that faced the equally pure white sofa. "I hope I didn't pay a decorator to do this," she said with a sweeping motion of her free hand. "This has got to be the most boring room I've ever seen. My hospital room at the trauma center was more cheerful than this antiseptic place."

"It suits . . . suited you," Chase said quietly.

Sam cringed. "Was I really that drab and dull?"

"You were never drab or dull."

Sam's heart fluttered slightly at the compliment, but she said nothing.

"You were just very precise, very organized. This would have appealed to your sense of neatness." His dark eyes narrowed slightly as they roamed over her face. Sam watched as he swallowed before speaking. "I—"

Whatever Chase was about to say was interrupted, yet again, by the ringing of the telephone. For a person just home, she certainly was in demand.

Chase rose, left the room and yelled to her from the kitchen, "Charlie Newsome and Karen Quinn are downstairs. Do you want to let them come up?"

"Please," she answered. If it had just been Charlie, Sam probably would have declined, but she would never dream of turning Karen away.

A few minutes later, Charlie entered the living room looking much as he had the last time Sam had seen him. Expensively tailored clothing hung from his slight shoulders. His sandy blond hair was perfectly styled and overmoussed. His greeting consisted of bending forward and kissing the air somewhere in the vicinity of her ear.

"You look great," he said with very little sincerity.

"Thanks," she returned. Karen gave her a hug that felt genuine. "Charlie, Karen, this is Chase Lawson. Chase is a friend from Gillian."

Charlie seemed to hesitate just a second before extending his hand. "From Gillian, you say?" he said.

"That's right," Chase informed him. He noted a slight tremor in the other man's hand, just as he thought he noticed a secretive communication between Charlie and the redhead. The woman appeared to be suddenly tense. She was definitely gripping the neatly wrapped present with enough pressure to dent the package.

"So," Charlie said as he stood stiffly in the middle of the room, "you're actually going to go through with this trip back to the wilds of Arizona?"

"Charlie!" Karen chastened.

Again Chase felt something strange pass between them.

"Are you sure you want to do this?" Karen asked Sam.

"I doubt you'll be able to jump-start your career if you take yourself out of circulation for too long," Charlie warned.

Chase watched Samantha's eyes dart between the two visitors. Her cheerful expression seemed to fade with each negative comment thrust at her. "I don't think I'm going to return to acting, Charlie. I told you that months ago."

"I wouldn't be so quick to kiss off a career—"

"But Charlie," Sam interrupted gently, "Karen told me she'll be my permanent replacement on *Secret Splendor*."

Chase noted the twitching vein at Charlie's throat and the hostile blue eyes he turned on the redhead.

"Well," Charlie said as he moved toward the door. "I guess our little Karen has filled you in, so we better be going. She's got an early call in the morning. Don't you, Karen?"

"What? I mean, yes, I do. An early call."

Karen quickly moved to follow the man, then stopped and pivoted toward Sam.

"I wanted to give you this." Karen held out the package.

With the gift presented to her, Sam appeared to choke with emotion. "You didn't have to do this," she protested as she slipped a fingernail beneath the tape that secured the gift wrap.

"It's nothing . . . Really," Karen insisted.

Chase found the man's behavior baffling. He was supposed to be one of Sam's friends, yet he obviously couldn't wait to get out the door. The way he was tugging at the redhead, Chase wondered if he'd let her stay long enough for Sam to thank her for the gift.

Chase moved closer to Sam as she lifted the lid of the box. It was more than just his desire to be next to her, it was the fact that she seemed confused by its contents. Peering over her shoulder into the box, he saw a simple, though expensive, gold chain tangled in the cotton. When she pulled it from the box, there was a small key dangling from the chain. The key was real, not an ornamental piece of jewelry.

"I'm . . . they found that key lying near you on the ground the night you were hurt. The cops gave it to me since you don't have any living relatives. You remember," she prodded Sam, "they gave me all the stuff they said they wouldn't need as evidence. It looks like the key to a jewelry box, or something. Anyway, I wanted to give it back to you just in case you decide to stay in Arizona. The necklace, of course, is so you won't forget me."

"That could never happen!" Sam exclaimed. "Thank you," she added in a smaller voice as she undid the clasp and attempted to place the delicate chain around her neck.

Chase's hands joined hers, nearly paralyzing him. He silently prayed that she wouldn't notice the effect she was having on him. *Not with so much at stake,* he added mentally. He felt a guilty smile form on his lips when he realized that the pulse at her throat had quickened in the time it had taken him to fasten the necklace.

Turning his attention back to the puzzling twosome, he found Karen's face beaming as she admired the chain and its less impressive-looking charm. Charlie looked bored to tears.

"Take care, kid. Keep in touch." Again, Charlie managed to kiss nothing but air around Sam's face.

The farewell between Sam and Karen was long and tearful and would have continued were it not for Charlie's throat-clearing intrusions, followed by even less subtle words of impatience. As Sam's visitors left the apartment, Chase wondered what an attractive woman like Karen was doing with a loser like Charlie.

"I don't mean to criticize," he began, trying to lighten her mood, "but I don't think a whole lot of your friend Charlie."

It worked. She flashed him a heart-stopping grin, her gray eyes sparkling with a mischievous light. "Nor do I," she assured him. "I can only speculate that he was a better agent than he is a human being. In the past several months, he hasn't exactly been a constant source of support in my life."

"Karen seemed nice," he said, hoping to draw her out.

It worked again. And Sam smiled as she filled him in on what a good friend Karen had been over the past year. Karen's loyalty struck Chase as rather odd—especially since Sam intimated that they, apparently, hadn't known each other all that well before the attack. Chase couldn't help wondering whether there was an ulterior motive behind Karen's alleged loyalty.

THEY HAD DINNER, and Chase used the time to formulate his next move. After the kitchen was returned to its original pristine condition, he put his plan into action.

"What would you think of going out for dessert?" he suggested, watching as her face lit up with excitement.

"There's one of those gourmet ice-cream shops a few blocks from here." After a brief flicker of indecision flashed through his mind, he told her, "I could use the fresh air. I'm not used to being cooped up like this. And you had that long drive this morning."

"You seem to forget, I'm an expert on being cooped up," she quipped as she retrieved her purse.

The early-evening air danced over her skin as she exited the building with Chase at her side. They followed the uneven sidewalk, their shadows from the glow of the streetlights splayed out in front of them.

As Sam studied their images on the pavement before her, she got the oddest feeling. It wasn't that annoying sensation she sometimes experienced of a memory bubbling just beneath the surface. This was something much different and far more frightening than anything she had encountered before.

"What's wrong?" Chase asked, moving in front of her. His hands shot out and gripped her upper arms. When she didn't answer immediately, she felt his fingers bite into the tender flesh of her arms.

Reaching up, she placed both palms flat against the solidness of his chest. Shaking her head, she felt the heat of embarrassment rise in her cheeks. "Nothing's wrong," she said with forced lightness. *I'm just making an absolute idiot of myself,* she told herself.

"If you're sure," he said before allowing his hands to drop.

"Positive," she assured him and quickened her pace. She reached the crosswalk before him and checked both directions for traffic.

She had just stepped off the curb when she heard Chase scream over the squealing sound of tires and the mechanical whine of a car engine. Sam spun around in response to the urgency in his tone, only to find herself blinded by the bright lights of a car barreling up the street. The stench of burning rubber assailed her nose, and the roar of the fast-approaching vehicle was near-deafening. Sam knew she had to react quickly, but somehow she wasn't getting the message to her frozen body. She opened her mouth to scream at the same instant the car jumped the curb and veered sharply in her direction.

Chapter Three

Suddenly, Sam felt her body rise into the air. Her arms and legs flailed helplessly for several seconds before the forces propelling her reversed and she began cascading downward. A sharp pain seared through the side of her body that connected with the pavement.

Her scream was silenced as her lungs collapsed from an immense weight crushing her from above. Her eyes closed instinctively against the next wave of torture. She was showered with bits of gravel, dirt and other debris as she heard the car's tires scraping the concrete curb.

Then the squeal of the tires rounding the corner pierced the quiet night air and was followed by an eerie silence. It was several seconds before the heaviness eased off her, allowing Sam to swallow a painful, tentative breath.

"Are you okay?" Chase asked.

"I think so," she answered, then cautiously turned over and gingerly pulled herself into a sitting position.

By the yellow glow of the streetlight, Chase ran his hands over her arms and legs, testing and examining each trembling extremity for possibly injury. It wasn't until he moved to her opposite side that Sam noticed the darkish stain beginning to form at the shoulder of his shirt.

"You're hurt!" she cried.

"It's just a scrape," Chase assured her, offering his hand and pulling her to her feet. His head darted from side to side as he scanned the street in both directions. "Come on," he said, placing one hand at her waist as he rushed to guide her back to the safety of the building.

"Oh, Chase," she said with concern. Once they were inside the elevator, she could see the deep scratches etched along his arm. The fabric of his shirt was little more than thin strips of crimson around his shoulder. "We should get you to a hospital!"

Chase chuckled softly. "It's not serious, Sam. Trust me."

"Trust you!" she exclaimed. "After what you just did, I think I owe you my firstborn child."

The smile on his face flickered, then quickly dimmed. "All I did was pull you out of the way."

Sam's attention remained on his injury. As the elevator opened on her floor, she found it impossible to dismiss what had just happened.

"That wasn't an accident, was it?"

Chase kept silent until they were safely in the apartment. He stood in the center of the living room, legs braced apart. She noted the stern, stark expression and the rapid rise and fall of his chest. She swallowed at the intensity she saw simmering in his eyes.

"Of course it was an accident," he said, though Sam didn't hear enough conviction to feel reassured.

She took a deep breath and willed herself not to panic. It had been close, but they were both safe. "Do you think we should call Detective Burns?" she asked softly. "After we have a look at your shoulder," she added when she saw resistance in his expression.

Reluctantly, Chase moved over to the phone. "Burns, first. I'll clean myself up while we wait for the cops."

Sam was beginning to be swayed by his casual handling of the whole affair. If he wasn't worried, there was no reason for her to be concerned.

After he had called the detective and filled him in, Chase shrugged out of his shirt.

"Nasty," Sam said when she saw the wound. She pulled him in the direction of the bathroom.

Leaving him perched against the marble sink, she went off in search of supplies. After a few minutes of searching, she managed to come up with a bottle of antiseptic and a roll of bandages. They weren't hard to find in the well-stocked hall closet, since the old Sam had arranged the shelves in alphabetical order.

The new Sam shook her head at such compulsiveness and found it impossible to relate to.

She reentered the bathroom only to discover that Chase had already taken a cloth and washed the worst of the dirt and grime from his injury.

"Horning in on my nursing debut?" she chided.

"Just doing what's necessary," he answered calmly.

Not quite sure what else to do, Sam stood by and watched as he cleansed the wound. He'd turned his torso at an angle. Everywhere she looked, Sam saw tight, rippling muscles encased in dark, smooth-looking skin. A silver chain dangled from his neck, and at the end of it hung a round, primitive emblem encrusted with brightly colored stones that formed a design in deep russet, turquoise and black. His body was absolutely perfect, as if a sculptor's hand had lovingly chiseled every inch of his impressive form. Her cheeks grew warm and she suddenly found she had difficulty breathing.

Still, as she walked towards him slowly, she found it impossible to drag her eyes away from the magnificent sight before her. She liked watching the wayward drop of water trickle down his chest, disappearing into the waistband of his jeans. Swallowing some of the tightness in her throat, she reached out to assist him and watched in fascination as the muscles of his stomach contracted with a sharp intake of his breath as she gently dabbed the medicine onto his cuts. A slow, but undeniably powerful warmth began to spread through her veins.

Forcing her eyes upward, Sam was startled to find him eyeing her with an amused, if not arrogant, grin. The buzz of the intercom saved her from having to think up some explanation for her blatant perusal of his body. Grateful for the interruption, she fled the bathroom with the sound of his soft chuckle echoing in her ears.

A few minutes after she had given her permission to the doorman, Detective Burns appeared in her doorway. His round face was wrinkled into accordion-like creases. When he inclined his head in a silent greeting, Sam's eye caught a momentary flash of brightness where the light reflected off his bald head.

Moving into the living room, the detective reached into the pocket of his drab raincoat and produced a tattered notepad. Sam wondered why everything he owned looked as if it had been accidentally run through the washing machine. His clothing was faded and could have benefited greatly from an introduction to an iron. What remained of his hair was a dull shade of brown, grown long on one side and then combed across the top of his head in an attempt to cover the pale circle of his scalp.

"Where's Chase?" he asked without preamble.

"In the bathroom. His shoulder was scraped up when we fell to the pavement."

But Sam wasn't thinking of his injury; in fact, her mind was having a hard time erasing the image of Chase bared to the waist. Shaking her head, she tried to rid herself of the vision.

Chase entered and sauntered toward them, pulling on a fresh, light blue shirt that was the perfect complement to his coloring.

Perhaps I was just a bit premature in leaving Greenhaven, Sam grumbled inwardly. Her sudden fascination with this man, particularly his body, was more threatening than the group therapy sessions on dream analysis.

"What happened?" Burns asked.

"A car tried to run us down," she said.

"Actually," Chase began as he gently lowered himself onto the sofa, "a car jumped the curb. Probably kids out joyriding."

Sam felt her mouth drop open. Chase was so calm and nonchalant in the telling that by the time he had repeated the details of the "incident," which it was now being called, Sam doubted her own recollections.

"It was an eighty-five or eighty-six, four door. Black, possibly maroon. Jersey plates, first three letters RDP."

Burns scooted over to the phone and called in the description. Sam was simply stupefied by Chase's recounting. The fact that he had kept his wits about him enough to take note of details about the car made her feel totally incompetent. It also made her feel like a fool for instantly jumping to the conclusion that some dark, evil force was out there lying in wait. Feeling silly, she excused herself by saying she wanted to wash up.

It wasn't until she closed her bedroom door behind her that Sam vented her frustration by kicking the white wicker trash basket, which toppled across the carpeting before coming to rest against one leg of the four-poster bed that dominated the room. Her gray eyes narrowed with fury and her breath came in short angry bursts.

"I feel like a fool!" she said between clenched teeth. "A car was chasing me," she mimicked. "They must think I'm a real idiot! What could I have been thinking?" She reached out and swatted the meticulously folded afghan that was draped over the back of the pristine white chaise. Stomping forward, she grabbed a handful of the white eyelet bedspread and tugged it out of position. "Get a grip, Sam!" she chided herself.

She was careful to keep her ranting voice down to a whisper, not at all certain how the two men in the other room would react to her tantrum. The last thing she wanted was an update on her mental state forwarded to Dr. Masters.

After briefly surveying the bedroom, a sense of calm slowly pervaded her system. Sam gained confidence from the knowledge that she could throw a first-class fit and not have several men in white coats to answer to. A smile curved the corners of her mouth. "Better," she decided. At least the room no longer looked like a shrine to the god of neatness, and her frazzled nerves had been somewhat soothed.

Sam changed into a pair of jeans and a mauve sweater. The stains on her discarded clothing looked beyond repair, so, impulsively, she righted the trash basket and stuffed the blouse and slacks inside before returning the wicker container to its proper place.

Satisfied, she went off to join the men. The carpet beneath her bare feet muffled the sound of her approach.

The detective's voice floated toward her. As the words became audible, Sam stopped and pressed herself flush against the wall. Ears straining, she was just barely able to make out their conversation.

" ... we still don't have any proof there's a connection."

"There's a connection." Chase's voice was so cold and final that a chill ran the length of her body.

"Let's hope—" The detective's sentence was cut off by a rapping at the front door.

Realizing she'd be discovered lingering in the shadows, Sam pushed herself away from the wall. Disappointment melded with guilt. She knew eavesdropping was rude, but it was also a good way to get information.

A uniformed officer, who looked to be about thirty, stood in the doorway, his forehead partially obscured by his hat. Bending forward, he whispered something into Detective Burns's ear that instantly produced a deep frown from the older officer.

Sam moved into the room and avoided eye contact with Chase. The subdued violence she'd heard in his voice had left her feeling somewhat wary. She could feel his dark eyes following her as she seated herself. His penetrating stare was nearly palpable in the tension-filled atmosphere.

"They recovered the car," Burns said to Chase.

"Is the driver in custody?" Sam asked hopefully.

The detective shook his head. "No. The car was abandoned in an alley about ten blocks from here. Stripped clean. It was reported stolen more than a year ago. Paperwork was filed and everything."

Sam felt a preliminary wave of relief wash over her. "So it really was an accident," she whispered. Instantly, her face burned from a blush. "I'm sorry to have called you out here," Sam added softly.

Burns shrugged and exchanged a look with Chase before reluctantly responding. "No problem. I'm sorry if what I said to you at Greenhaven yesterday has you spooked."

"It's just my paranoia surfacing, Detective," she assured him with a small smile. "I'm sorry someone had their car stripped, but that's good for me, isn't it?" she asked.

Chase cleared his throat. "It appears that this was nothing more than you and me being at the wrong place at the wrong time. Just a couple of thieves taking a car out for a test drive before relieving it of its marketable parts."

Burns nodded his agreement, but Sam sensed something hollow about the action. "The lab boys are on their way down there now. Who knows?" he said, shrugging. "Maybe the robbery detail will get lucky."

Burns departed with the promise that he would call them in Arizona if a search of the car revealed anything. Something in his tone told Sam he wasn't terribly optimistic.

With Burns gone, the apartment seemed to shrink around her. Chase's presence loomed over her like a thundercloud rumbling over the horizon. He appeared tense, each movement stiff and measured. He paced the confines of the room, his hands shoved deep inside the pockets of his jeans. His open shirt flapped against his chest, drawing her eyes to the vast expanse of richly colored skin beneath.

Thinking that a distraction might help them both, Sam returned to her bedroom and threw open the double doors of the closet.

Several staggered rows of expensive clothing stared back at her, some encased in cleaner's plastic, while others were zipped into clear vinyl bags for protection. Ignoring the fact that the clothes were arranged by color, style and purpose, she stood on tiptoe to grasp one of three large boxes on an upper shelf.

Sam gave a startled squeal as the box tilted too far forward, showering her with some of its contents.

"You okay?" Chase asked, appearing in the bedroom doorway and rushing to assist her.

"Fine. The top came off as I was trying to get it down."

"Here," he said as he came up behind her. "Let me help."

Sam didn't respond with words, her body was far too busy reacting to the feel of his thighs as they brushed against her backside. When he lifted his arms above her head as he reached for the box, Sam swallowed hard. Tight, rock-solid muscles pressed against her back, molding his outstretched body to hers.

"Is this all you want?"

"Excuse me?" she squeaked.

"Is this the only box you want down?"

Sam nodded, not daring to speak for fear it would be in that embarrassing, high-pitched voice that made her sound like some pathetic, sex-starved idiot.

Maybe that's exactly what I am, she thought as she waited for him to back up before she attempted to move. Perhaps her head injury had caused her to regress into behaving like a libidinous adolescent. She found the notion quite disconcerting.

Chase deposited the box on her bed while Sam gathered the items that had fallen. As she approached the bed, she found him staring at the neatly labeled folders with one dark eyebrow arched in apparent disbelief.

"I think you missed your calling," he said dryly.

"Really?"

One finger flicked a color-coded label neatly typed and attached to a color-coordinated divider. "I've never seen anything like this. It's incredible!"

Sam felt warmth spread over her cheeks. "I know what you mean. The first time I saw the way everything was *so* organized, I was a little shocked."

Chase began reading the labeled partitions. "Gifts, 1976...Mementos, 1976...Homework, 1976—"

"I know, I know," Sam interrupted. "It's like that for every year of my life."

"Whew," he whistled softly. "When we get back home, remind me to give you my checkbook to balance. You've got one hell of a talent for organization."

"Compulsive overkill, you mean," she quipped. "But, I will admit all this may turn out to be a blessing in disguise. I'm probably the only amnesiac on record with all the fragments of her life cataloged and color-coded."

Sam noticed that his dark eyes had suddenly gone cloudy again. It was like watching the last sliver of sun fade into oblivion. In a flash, however, the guarded look was gone, replaced by one of overt curiosity.

"So what exactly have you got in here?"

Sam and Chase sat on the bed, the box between them. "I seem to recall that my high school yearbook is stashed in here someplace. If you don't mind, I would appreciate a review of the people I know in Gillian." Her fingers ruffled through the compartments, a look of determination sharpening the angle of her chin.

"Try looking there," Chase suggested, pointing to a specific year.

The small leather volume was sandwiched between several yellowed programs. When she extracted the book, crumbled bits of dried flowers floated down into the box. Sam looked into the bottom and discovered it contained quite a collection of wilted and petrified corsages in varying degrees of decay.

"Did I ever throw anything away?" she groaned.

"Obviously not."

Gillian High was embossed across the front of the gray cover in bright blue block letters. Beneath that, the year was printed in a smaller, complementary type.

The book smelled of leather, and the spine made a crackling sound as she turned to the first page. Handwritten messages nearly obscured the photograph of what she knew must be the school building.

Moving the box to the floor, Chase slid close enough so that he, too, could see the pages of the yearbook. Suddenly, his proximity made Sam wish she would have suggested taking the book into the living room. She found it difficult to concentrate with him so close. When he shifted slightly, his bulk forced them even closer. Her arms and legs brushed against his with disturbing frequency.

Try as she might, Sam found the situation impossible. Chase dominated her peripheral vision, and her mind could focus on nothing other than the pleasant but torturous sight of his partially exposed chest. *This isn't working!* she finally admitted to herself.

"I think I'd like a glass of water. Let's take this stuff into the kitchen," she said hoarsely. Snapping the book closed, Sam jumped from the bed.

She stopped suddenly in the doorway, her back stiff, her shoulders squared. For all the bravado in her stance, she couldn't muster the nerve to turn and face him as she spoke.

"Chase?"

"Yes?"

"Please button your shirt."

WHAT STARTED AS a slow, amused smile grew broader as Chase absently did as she requested. He knew he'd been playing a dangerous game with her. Still, his ego liked the fact that in spite of her failed memory, she wasn't immune to him.

You are a real heel! he thought admonishingly as he tucked the box under one arm, balancing the weight on his hip. What kind of man was he, anyway? *A normal, healthy one,* he answered silently and felt a wicked smile curl his lips.

He found her gulping down a drink. There was just the slightest tremble in the hand she used to raise the glass to her lips. Her eyes seemed much wider than he remembered. Grayer, wider and more expressive, though her most common expression these days appeared to linger somewhere between caution and anxiety. She looked so small and fragile.

Quite to the contrary, she was apparently one strong lady. Sam had made it through the brutal attack in the park, and had then somehow managed to pull through the months of painful mental and physical therapy in order to try to piece her life back together. Why then, he wondered, did he feel such a fierce, overpowering need to protect her...even from himself? They could never go back. Even before all this happened, Chase had long ago accepted that Sam wasn't going to be a part of his life. Or had he?

The thought brought a fierce frown to his face.

"If you don't want to do this, you don't have to," she said in obvious reaction to his expression.

"No problem, really." Depositing the box on the table, Chase settled himself in one of the chairs. Forcing a smile, he willed himself to ignore the way her sweater clung appealingly to every sensual curve of her body. He'd been crazy to get involved. Only a glutton for punishment would let himself get caught up in something like this!

Spotting the corner of an envelope sticking out of the yearbook, Chase reached out and, in the process, his hand brushed the back of hers. Startled by the unexpected contact, not to mention the silky smoothness of her skin, Chase jerked his hand back. "Sorry."

Sam had also pulled away, folding her hands in her lap to allow his hand an unobstructed path to the book. With the tip of one finger, he removed the yellowed envelope.

Inside, he discovered a collection of candid pictures, some as old as fifteen years. He recognized everyone, feeling his gut clench as he scanned the smiling adolescent faces in the photographs.

His expression must have alarmed her, for Sam came around and peered over his shoulder.

"That's me," she said in a soft, detached voice. As she reached to place a finger against the image, he was forced to endure the sweet torture of having the curves of her body pressed tightly against his back. Sheer determination kept him from groaning aloud.

"And that's you!" she said with a bit more enthusiasm. "Look at your hair!" Her giggles filled the small space between them.

Chase did groan audibly then. The military-style crew cut made his ears look like wings that had sprouted from either side of his head. "This was taken the summer after graduation. I was in between boot camp and Germany."

"How old were we?"

"You were seventeen. I was twenty."

Sam backed away and said, "But I thought you and I were the same age."

Turning, he smiled at the guarded expression in her eyes. "You were something of an academic wonder. I was a behavior problem." When she looked perplexed by his explanation, Chase continued, "I wasn't exactly what you would call a model student. They figured if I stayed back a few times, I might get the hang of it. Consequently, I repeated a few grades."

Sam nodded and returned her attention to the picture. "Who's this? He looks a lot like you."

"That's Cody. He's my brother. He recently got married, although that hasn't seemed to cure him of his overbearing, macho personality."

"And you aren't macho and overbearing?"

He chuckled softly. "I prefer to think of myself as physically active and assertive."

"I don't know," Sam said on a sigh. "You don't exactly fit the profile of the new beta male image I've heard so much about."

"Beta male?"

"The sensitive, caring man who places importance on the emotional side of relationships. He marries, changes diapers—that sort of thing."

Chase tossed his head back and laughed in earnest. "Where on earth did you hear all this garbage?"

She crossed her arms in front of her chest and glared at him. Her lips were pursed in what he assumed to be an affronted pout. It made him wonder what her mouth would feel like beneath his.

"Talk shows."

"Just so I understand this correctly, your knowledge of male-female relationships is based on watching television talk shows?" he said, laughing again.

"Don't laugh at me!"

"I'm sorry, Sam. Really." Clearing his throat, he swallowed the last of his laughter. By the way her eyes had narrowed into slits of sparkling silver, it was apparent that she wasn't enjoying his amusement.

She sighed heavily before returning her attention to the picture. "Who's this?"

"Grace Morningdew." Saying the name caused his body to stiffen with emotion. The tense feeling only worsened when he dared to peek at the smiling brunette, her dark eyes shining up from the picture.

Anticipating her next question, he tapped the last face in the picture and said, "Patricia Sands."

"Where are we in this picture?"

"The backyard of Gran's house. And it had to be some time near the middle of the summer, 'cause I shipped out in late July."

"What were we doing?"

"You threw me a going-away party." Chase carefully measured each syllable of his response. They had taken great pains to warn him against revealing anything to her that wasn't calculated to result in the success of their plan.

"Was it fun?"

"Yes." He found himself smiling somewhat sadly. She might not remember, but he did. *Brother, did he ever!*

"It looks like we were all close friends."

"Some closer than others."

He looked up to find yet another blush painting her cheeks the same rosy hue as her mouth, and he felt guilty for making the remark.

"I'm sure it's weird for you that I don't remember anything about . . . us—"

"It's okay," he cut in. His eyes purposefully went to the faces staring back at him from the photograph. "You're right. We were all good, close friends."

"Then why do I hear such sadness in your voice?"

"Do you?" he responded vaguely, afraid of where the conversation was headed.

Her fingers pressed against his upper arm, forcing him to look into her eyes. Quietly, he studied her features.

"I'm not sad. I'm just reminiscing about the past. I suppose there is always some regret when you look back on your youth."

He watched a wide range of emotions play across her face and found himself holding his breath. He should never have allowed this little trek down memory lane—especially when he knew full well what was waiting at the end of the road. What he didn't know was how to anticipate her reaction.

"But, just think, in less than a week you'll be seeing all these people again at the reunion," she said.

He smiled wanly at the cheerful quality of her voice. "Maybe not as many as you might think." He hoped she'd let his cryptic remark pass. She didn't.

Sam touched her finger to each face in the photograph as she spoke. "Why not? Don't you think Patricia and Grace will attend? Have they left Gillian?"

"In a manner of speaking."

"Chase!" she said emphatically, frustration marring her pretty features. "What do you mean 'in a manner of speaking'?"

"They won't be there."

"Why not?"

"They're both dead."

Chapter Four

"We should be in Gillian in about an hour."

"And what do you propose to do once you get here?"

"I'll take care of her."

"You'd better. You really blew it in New York. I'm not paying for mistakes, I'm paying for results!"

"And you'll get them. This isn't like planning a party, damn it! If you want speed, I can do it sloppy."

"It has to look like an accident. That's what we agreed. If her death is investigated, I'll lose everything. And if I go down, I'll take you with me. I can promise you that."

"Don't worry. I'll take care of your problem. Accidents are my specialty. That's why I'm so expensive."

"You've already had two opportunities and you've blown them both."

"Unfortunate incidents."

"I don't want unfortunate incidents. I want her dead. And fast!"

CHASE LOOKED AT HER out of the corner of his eye as he leaned his body in between the privacy shields on either side of the pay telephone. The noise in the terminal made it impossible for him to carry on his conversation, but he had heard enough to know what his latest edict was. He felt his mood grow dark and serious beneath the shadow of the Stetson pulled low on his forehead. He agreed, even though in his gut he knew there were problems with the feasibility of the plan. Who was he kidding? he thought as he squeezed the dead receiver against his ear. The thought of what he was being forced to do to Sam only served to stir the simmering brew of frustration in the pit of his stomach. "I guess I really don't have a choice," he whispered into the phone.

LETTING OUT an impatient sigh as she waited for Chase to finish his phone call her attention wavered to the scenes unfolding around her. Instantly, she became aware of just how out of place she looked in her silk suit and pumps. Everyone else was wearing jeans, casual shirts and boots. Chase's chambray shirt and jeans were black, but at least he blended with the crowd.

Annoyed by the warmth moistening her palms, she turned her attention back to where he stood at the long bank of phones. Though hardly in a position to dictate his activities, Sam felt a tad perturbed at the way he'd left her just standing there. She knew it was silly, but she couldn't help feeling abandoned. The stares and muffled whispers of passersby made her feel like some sort of freak on display in a sideshow.

More than one person had slowed or pointed at her, sometimes sharing a comment with a companion. Sighing, she hoped their rudeness was due to her relative infamy and not her bright pink suit. Disgustedly, she looked down at her custom-made, dyed-to-match pink pumps.

"It's hard to fade into the woodwork when you're dressed from head to toe in fuchsia," she grumbled.

"What's that?"

Her head shot up, and her expression melted into a relieved smile. "Fashion commentary."

He wrinkled his forehead. "Come again?"

"Forget it. Ready?"

When Chase reached out for her arm, Sam experienced a strange sensation. The feel of his callused fingers against the fabric of her clothing seemed somehow familiar.

"You can wait at the curb while I get my car out of long-term parking."

Sam swallowed her protest, not wishing to appear frightened and paranoid as she had after the incident with the car yesterday.

Her first breath of Arizona air was not at all what she had expected. Warm, polluted air filled her lungs as she watched Chase's back disappear into the cav-

ernous mouth of the parking garage. Holding her
purse tightly against her side, Sam looked around. She
was surprised to find herself in a deserted loading area.
"Thank you, Chase," she grumbled amid the echoes
of cars passing on the overhead ramp.

"Be calm," she told herself. In spite of the long
shadows, it was daylight. "Nothing bad happens during the daytime."

A loud sound made her jump. Turning, she looked
toward the sound and found that a dark figure had
emerged from a set of double doors about fifty feet
from where Chase had left her.

"Don't overreact," she told her slightly trembling
body as her eyes began to examine the mysterious figure.

He was forty feet away. She was fairly certain it was
a man, though it was hard to get an exact reading on
his height when her only references were tall, tiled pil-
lars supporting the roadway above. With each successive step the stranger took, Sam heard the pounding
of her heart in her ears begin to eclipse the deafening
sound of the traffic. He was still coming.

He was thirty feet away. *Where are you Chase?* she
thought nervously as she chanced a look toward the
garage. It seemed to her as if some unknown force had
lifted the adjacent building and moved it miles away
from where she stood. The feeling of isolation only
fueled her burgeoning sense of dread. He was coming
closer.

He was twenty feet away. The hood of a black sweatshirt was pulled up over his head, his features completely hidden by the ominous-looking shroud. Her instincts kicked into overdrive as she suddenly realized why his attire bothered her. It had to be near eighty degrees, and the man coming near her was wearing a heavy sweat suit, gloves and dark hiking boots. And he was still coming.

He was ten feet away. *C'mon, Chase!* she silently implored.

When the hooded figure reached into the front pouch of his sweatshirt, Sam made her decision. With genuine alarm propelling her, she made a dash for the garage. The staccato sound of her heels on the pavement joined the pounding of her heart, reverberating the fear in her brain. Barely noticing that she'd dropped her purse, Sam used both hands to pry open the heavy door to the parking area. Just before going inside, she chanced a glance over her shoulder and saw that he was still coming.

There was row after row of cars, but no people. It was eerily quiet, save for the sound of her labored breathing and footsteps. She heard the sound of metal scraping against concrete, and Sam knew the stranger had entered the dimly lit garage, as well. Her chest felt heavy with terror as she weaved her crouched form through the web of cars.

Bent behind a beat-up truck, Sam peered through the dirty windows. He was still coming. When she moved, he moved, and she realized that he was tracking her.

Not knowing what else to do, she slipped off her pumps and slid them under one of the cars. The floor was cool and damp in places as she moved from row to row, always mindful to keep her pursuer in sight. No matter which direction she chose, he seemed to counter her every move. His pace never quickened, not even in response to the frenetic movements Sam was making in the hopes of outdistancing him. He was only two rows away from her... and she was running out of room.

To her horror, she realized, too late, that she had worked herself into the worst possible position. There were only three rows in front of her, the last abutted a concrete wall. And he was still coming.

She was about to scream when he reached for something in the pocket of his sweatshirt. He was close enough now that Sam could tell he was huge. Suddenly—too suddenly—the only thing that separated them was a battered compact.

Without ever removing his hood, the man slowly pulled his gloved hand from his shirt. He moved without sound. Something metal caught the reflection of the floodlight behind her. Her hand flew to her mouth, trying in vain to coax some sound from her paralyzed throat.

Closing her eyes and replaying the scene in her mind, Sam felt as if she were watching his motions frame by frame. It seemed as if it took him several minutes to pull the object from the concealment of his clothing. Sam flung herself backward, until her shoulder collided with the hard wall. She opened her eyes slowly, fully expecting to see a gun or a knife. She was surprised to see, instead, a set of keys dangling from his forefinger.

"Keys?" she said in a choked voice.

He never looked at her. He simply allowed the small ring to hang from his gloved finger before he swore under his breath, then turned abruptly and sprinted through the cars. Sam collapsed to the floor. She hugged herself, hoping to calm the rapid pulse that made her feel too shaky to stand.

"Keys," she said again. Her voice was muffled by the sound of an engine starting. "I ran for no reason," she said, chuckling with relief. She was stupefied at the way her mind had magnified what was obviously an innocent incident. "Chase will have me committed."

Chase. Praying she would be able to salvage her dignity, Sam rose and began searching for her hastily discarded pumps. "They have to be here." She kept searching but to no avail—she had to get back outside and wait for Chase. The last thing she wanted was to have to explain to him why she had run off. "Damn," she grumbled when it became apparent that she would have to get down on all fours on the filthy concrete in order to find her shoes. But she needed to get lower still, so there was no alternative but to lie flat in order to survey the garage floor.

Careful to avoid oil spots, Sam lay down and her eyes began scanning beneath the cars. She spotted her shoes about three cars over, stood and quickly ran to retrieve them.

She was kneeling with her left arm under a Volvo when she felt a large hand claw her jacket. She screamed and rolled in an attempt to throw her attacker off balance. It was a good idea, but she hadn't counted on him sprawling on top of her as he fell. Sam grunted as the wind was forced from her lungs. Tears flooded her eyes.

"It's me!"

It took a full second for the voice to register in her frazzled brain. She closed her eyes and warm tears spilled over her cheeks. Her back hurt from having his full weight on top of her. The ground was hard and cold, and she pushed at him in an attempt to get some air into her lungs.

"Sam?" Chase wasn't quite prepared for the sight before him. There were smudges of grease and dirt on her face and clothes. Once standing, he easily pulled her to her feet. "Sam?" he repeated.

"I'm okay," she said in a raspy whisper.

"Well you don't look okay," he told her as he steadied her shaking form. "What happened?"

"Field trip."

"Do you always leave your purse behind when you wander off?"

She looked up at him with those big gray eyes brimming with tears, and he just about gave in to his instincts, which were screaming for him to pull her into his arms.

"I made a small error in judgment," she told him after averting her eyes.

"And what was that?"

"You'll think I'm crazy if I tell you."

"No, I won't," he assured her. "You're as pale as a ghost. What spooked you?"

Suddenly, Chase wanted to shake an answer out of her but knew his impatience would only hinder his purpose. It took an immeasurable amount of self-control for him to allow her to adjust her clothing and find her shoes without demanding the details.

"I guess Detective Burns has made me suspicious of every person I see."

"Meaning?"

"I thought some guy was following me."

"You what?" He stopped her, turning her slender shoulders until they stood toe-to-toe. There was a faint blush on her smudged cheeks, and she kept her eyes downcast.

"I saw this man in black, and I panicked and ran in here, thinking the devil himself was on my heels."

"Back up," Chase told her in a voice he struggled to keep calm. "Tell me about the man in black."

"There's nothing to tell," she assured him as she shrugged out of his grasp. "He was just going to his car, and I made a total idiot of myself. Just like last night."

"What do you mean, just like last night?"

"When I insisted that you call Burns. I could tell he didn't appreciate being called for no reason."

"What about the man, Sam? Was he blond? Dark-haired?"

"I couldn't tell."

"Couldn't tell?"

"He had his hood pulled over his head."

Chase held his breath and then let it out slowly as they walked back to where he had abandoned his car. She was hugging the purse Chase had returned to her, and she was obviously traumatized by the incident. But there wasn't a damn thing he could do about it.

The sound of his booted heels hitting the pavement echoed in the concrete cavern of the parking area, drowning out the sound of her pumps. Chase led her out the door to a brown Land Rover and helped her into the passenger seat. When his hand pressed gently against her backside, Sam leaped forward as if she'd been speared. Chase pretended not to notice and took his place behind the wheel.

"You might as well relax, Gillian's a good hour's drive from here," Chase mentioned as he slowed to pay an attendant at the exit of the lot.

"I'm fine," she lied, forcing a smile to her lips.

He cast her a sidelong glance before forcing the car into gear.

FEIGNING A SUDDEN fascination with topography, Sam kept her head turned away from him. Confined to such a small space seemed to emphasize everything about him, as well as the tattered, grungy appearance of her clothing. Sam could hear the even sound of his breathing over the twangy country music playing on the radio. She swallowed, hoping to redirect any personal thoughts regarding him. Sam took some tissues out of her purse and busied herself with wiping away the smudges of dirt and grime on her hands and face.

The sun beat down mercilessly on the shimmering desert, where scattered mesquite occasionally broke the monotony of parched, yellowish sand. In the distance, she saw multicolored buttes and vistas and the occasional verdant squares of irrigated farmland.

"This is really different from New York!"

Chase chuckled softly, probably at the childish wonder in her gushing exclamation. She felt her face warm as an adolescent blush punctuated her high-pitched tone.

"This is beautiful country," he said.

"Yes," she agreed. "It is." Shifting her position, she turned at an angle to face his profile. And schooling herself in self-control, she tried not to think about what an attractive profile it was. "You want to tell me about Grace and Patricia?"

His eyebrows wrinkled immediately, and she noted a slight tightening of the bronzed fingers that gripped the wheel. "I don't think getting into all that is such a good idea. I probably shouldn't have told you anything in the first place. You seemed really spooked last night."

"I'll admit that hearing it last night was a bit of a shock," she explained in a calm but determined voice. "But now that I've digested what you told me, I'd like to know the details."

Impatiently, she waited, watching the indecision play across his features. After a deep sigh, Chase simply said, "Like I said, they're dead."

"How?" Sam shifted again, pressing herself against the backrest and folding one nylon-clad leg beneath her slender body. Her hands reached down to grip the sides of the seat, but her eyes remained fixed on the pained expression she read on his face.

"Accidents," he said. There was reluctance in his tone and a further stiffening in his spine.

"Accidents? Car accidents? What?"

One hand reached up and raked through the neatly styled strands of ebony hair. "Patty died when the radio fell into her bathtub at her apartment in San Diego."

"What was she doing in San Diego?"

"That's where she lived." As he turned to look at her briefly, she noticed that the expression in his eyes had grown solemn.

"And Grace?"

He hesitated a second or two before saying, "Hit and run."

Her breath stalled in her throat. "Like what happened to us yesterday?"

Chase adamantly shook his head. "Nothing like that. You heard Burns." His mouth curved into a lazy half smile that returned some of the sparkle to his eyes.

Sam rubbed her hands along her arms, hugging away the chill that his revelations had produced. "I guess that sounded pretty paranoid of me, huh?"

"No, it's my fault. I shouldn't have sprung all that on you so soon after—"

"Don't do that, Chase," Sam interrupted. "Don't treat me like I'm unbalanced. Even if I do run from innocent men in broad daylight."

Quickly he raised his hands in mock surrender before returning them to the wheel. He turned and winked before saying, "Deal."

"Were there investigations into these accidents?"

"Yes," he assured her in a flat tone.

"And?"

"And nothing. They were accidents. Period."

"You don't sound convinced."

She watched the muscles in his forearms contract with tension, though he donned a broad grin when he glanced, briefly, in her direction. "Now you *are* sounding paranoid."

Sheepishly, Sam turned and faced forward in her seat. He was right—and her logical side assured her of that. Still, there was something unsettling about so many "accidents."

The miles rolled by with nothing but occasional polite banter between them. Little by little, the barren landscape gave way to a modest suburban sprawl.

Chase navigated through a small town at the foot of some mountains. When he finally stopped the car in front of one particular house, the first thing Sam noticed was that everything was done in shades of brown. The adobe-style, single-story home was a pale tan that threatened to fade into obscurity set against the backdrop of barren mountains.

Her eyes fixed on the house, which was protected by a low fence and set a few yards back from the road. Reaching for the door handle, Sam froze in mid-action.

"You okay?"

Accepting the hand he held out for her, Sam nodded and plastered a smile on her face. His hand was big and warm and managed to fill her with a comforting sense of calm.

While Chase gathered their luggage from the car, she passed through the decorative archway leading to a stone-edged garden. She stopped suddenly to allow a small lizard the right-of-way.

"Sorry," Chase mumbled as his body bumped hers.

Glancing at him over her shoulder, Sam smiled dismissively. The sound of his deep voice echoed in her ears, and the skin of her back felt heated beneath the fabric of her blouse where his body had touched hers. For a brief second, an electric sort of tension filled the inches that separated them in the small enclosed courtyard.

Swallowing hard, she forced her sluggish feet forward until she stood, expectantly, in front of a massive pair of polished wooden doors.

Reaching around her, Chase's dark hand maneuvered a key into the lock, turning it until the faint sound of the tumblers disengaging signaled success.

The first thing she noticed was the unmistakable scent of freshly cut flowers. Following the fragrance, Sam spied a large ceramic vase perched atop the coffee table, virtually overflowing with white blossoms. Excitedly, she moved forward and plucked a tiny card from among the roses. "Welcome home," she read aloud. Her forehead wrinkled in a frown when she flipped the card over and found no signature. Turning, she found Chase lingering by the door, a broad smile on his face. His expression erased her frown. "You?" she asked.

"White roses were always one of your favorites," he said nonchalantly.

"Thank you."

"It was nothing," Chase insisted, his head bowed slightly.

"You're wrong," Sam countered as she tossed her handbag onto the sofa and slipped the card into the pocket of her jacket.

A barely discernible blush rose on his high cheekbones.

"It was a nice thing for you to do, and I appreciate the gesture." It was apparent that her words of thanks were making him even more uncomfortable. Chase hadn't budged from the doorway. Their eyes met for a second in a powerful, nonverbal exchange that sent a jolt through her system.

One hand grasped the navy duffel that she knew was his only piece of luggage. His other hand was weighted down by the designer tapestry satchel that Sam had hurriedly packed earlier that morning.

"Here, I'll take mine."

"Nope, I'll just go ahead and take it in to your bedroom," Chase insisted.

Sam followed him down the hall, her eyes curiously peeking into each open door they passed along the way. Judging from the number and decor of the rooms, her grandmother had lived a comfortable existence.

Chase waited off to the left of a door near the end of the hall and said, "After you."

"Goodness!" Sam exclaimed before her hand managed to cover her mouth. The room was a near replica of the white mausoleum that was her New York apartment.

"Look at it this way," Chase suggested as he stepped around her to place her bag on the bed, "at least you were consistent."

"Consistently dull," she grumbled.

"It's not that bad," he said after one quick look around.

"You're right, it's not bad. It's just *so* white."

She could see the laughter in his eyes and found it contagious.

He moved toward her, until the feel of his breath washed over her face in warm waves. Tilting her head back, Sam searched his eyes beneath the thick outline of his lashes.

"I think we need to get this out of the way," he said gruffly.

Bending at the waist, Chase leaned forward until his lips barely grazed hers. Wide-eyed, Sam experienced the first tentative motions of the kiss through a haze of surprise. As the pressure from his mouth increased, growing slightly more insistent with each passing second, she found herself bombarded with an artillery of conflicting emotions.

His hands moved slowly, carefully, to her small waist. His strong fingers slipped beneath the fabric of her jacket and came to rest just beneath the swell of her rib cage. Her brain struggled as urgent messages swam against currents of curiosity, desire and just the faintest bit of apprehension.

Her mouth burned where he incited fires with the gentle prodding of his tongue, an involuntary gasp rising in her throat at the heady new sensations pulsing through her system. When he moved even closer, the feel of his thighs brushing hers was almost as intoxicating as the kiss itself. The heat from his mouth washed over her entire body, until every nerve ending tingled with a fierce life of its own.

Chase lifted his head for the fraction of a second it took to wrap his arms more tightly around her, as he lifted her up and against him. Fortified by her newly awakened desire, Sam moved her hands across the vast expanse of his chest and then around the taut muscles, until she was able to feel the solidness of his back. Arching herself slightly, she held her breath in anticipation of something unknown.

Whatever she'd expected, it wasn't the knocking sound that suddenly reverberated through the house. Chase all but jumped away from her, his breath coming in deep, ragged spurts.

As the pounding on the door became more insistent, Sam felt her cheeks grow warm with a guilty blush. The air between them sizzled, and their eyes locked. Reaching blindly behind her, she clung to one of the bedposts. Sam was certain that the strong desire she had just experienced had melted her kneecaps into uselessness.

"Sam, I . . ." His voice trailed off, lost as yet another wave of pounding echoed through the room.

Forcing a smile to her lips, she silently prayed that her expression betrayed none of the emotions warring inside her still-trembling body.

"We'd better get that," she suggested. Chase's nod was barely perceptible and a heavy frown burrowed deep crevices into the tanned flesh of his broad forehead.

She allowed her eyes to follow the gentle dip of his shoulders as she followed him down the hall toward the door. Softly, she cursed his composure and—while she was at it—she cursed herself, as well. The word *swoon* filtered into her brain. She'd read that word time and time again in books but never really understood its meaning—until now.

Girlish squeals of delight split through the air just seconds before two women bounded through the door and surrounded Chase. Sam judged them to be about her age, a blonde and a dark-haired woman, whose features and coloring seemed vaguely familiar.

"Sam!" the blonde yelped as she flung her arms around Sam, nearly toppling her onto the couch. "What happened to you? Did Chase make you ride on the luggage rack?"

"Very funny," she heard him say. "Sam had a small misadventure at the airport. Nothing serious."

A second pair of arms joined in with the first, and Sam felt herself being bounced into a group hug. The blonde's heavy perfume replaced the pleasant scent of Chase's cologne and the unpleasant recollection of the incident at the airport.

When the women stepped back, Sam searched their faces but discovered not even a hint of recognition. Not fully trusting what her reaction should be, Sam looked to Chase.

A warm smile had transformed his face. His dark eyes sparkled with obvious pleasure as he scanned the group.

"This is Mildred," he said as he moved forward and placed a hand on the blond woman's shoulder, "and Connie," he continued. "I made the mistake of telling them we'd be getting in today." It was obvious the censure in his remark carried little weight with the women.

"We're your welcoming committee!" Mildred announced. Taking her thumb and forefinger, she lifted Chase's hand and tossed it away from her shoulder as if it were nothing more than an annoying insect.

"Absolutely," Connie said gleefully.

Their smiles faded as they took in the blank expression on her face. Squeezing through the women, Chase stood at her side, his arm protectively at her waist.

Connie's features were large and exotic, accentuated by the slight bulging of her pouting lower lip. Conversely, Mildred had an air of naturalness that made her seem far more accessible. Sam's tentative smile appeared to placate the two women.

"I appreciate your coming by," she said softly.

"Wouldn't have missed it for the world," Mildred said.

"Besides," Connie said, leaning forward to deliver the words in a stage whisper, "we were sure you'd be sick to death of Chase by now."

"She likes me," Chase said with a mock-defensive tone.

"That's always been one of your problems, Lawson," Mildred injected. "*Too* many women like you."

Sam watched as he shifted from foot to foot, their taunts apparently making him uncomfortable.

Connie inched forward and placed a well-manicured hand on Sam's upper arm. "I've got an idea," she said brightly. "Chase, be a dear and run down to The Well. Bring back a couple bottles of wine and some snacks."

"Good idea," Mildred said. "We'll stay here with Sam."

She watched as Chase looked skeptically from one woman to the other, obviously unsure of what to do.

Feeling like little more than a child, Sam cleared her throat and said, "Please go, Chase. I'll be fine with Mildred and Connie."

"Are you sure?"

She pasted a smile on. "I really am capable of taking care of myself." When he still didn't dare make a move toward the door, she added, "And I promise not to play with any sharp objects or the electrical appliances."

Smiling after the playful wink she had used to punctuate her remark, he spun and left the house. A triumphant smile lingered at the corners of Sam's mouth.

"Well, now that he's gone, we can gossip," Connie said.

Sam found the prospect intriguing, and she demonstrated her willingness to at least listen by leading the two women to the sofa. Seating herself in an overstuffed chair with a large floral print, Sam kicked off her heels and tucked her legs beneath her, tugging down the hem of her skirt in the process. Mildred and Connie sat directly across from her on the sofa, their faces camouflaged by shadows reflecting through atrium doors to their left.

"Has being here triggered any memories?" Mildred asked.

Shaking her head, Sam answered, "Nothing of any consequence." But the memory of Chase's mouth on hers brought a warm, tingling sensation to her lips.

"Then we'll just have to set about making some new memories for you," Connie said.

Sam watched the dark-haired woman, surprised at how comfortable she was beginning to feel around these women.

"So, what's it like being around Chase after all this time?" Mildred asked.

Sam was taken aback by the question and not at all certain how to respond. Given the blazing curiosity she read in Mildred's eyes, she decided to offer some sort of answer. "He's a very unique man."

Mildred nodded vigorously, but it was Connie's I-know-something-you-don't-know smile that drew Sam's attention.

"Connie, you look like you're about to burst. Is there something about Chase you'd like to tell me?"

"Yes."

"No!" Mildred's solid protest all but drowned out the other woman's response.

Sam became a spectator as Mildred and Connie volleyed stern looks at each other.

"Look," Sam said as she expelled her breath. "If there's something going on here I should know about, I think it would be better to get it all out in the open."

Good Lord, I sound just like Dr. Masters! Sam thought exasperatedly.

"Now see what you've started, Connie!" Mildred groaned as she scrambled to her feet. She reached Sam's side and patted her on the shoulder. "I thought we decided—"

"No. *You* decided," Connie said emphatically.

"This is supposed to be a *pleasant* visit," Mildred warned.

"Well, I think she's got a right to know. After all, he's all but moved in here."

"Sam has a right to know *facts*." Mildred's voice had risen to somewhere dangerously close to a screech. "And you don't have any facts, Connie. So don't poison Sam's mind with your paranoid ramblings."

"I'm right at home with paranoid ramblings," Sam interjected. "A year in a sanatorium will do that to you."

The two women stopped bickering, their faces frozen in expressions of shock.

Connie's oval face blossomed into a broad grin. "I swear, Sam. That sounded like something you would have said years ago."

Sam's expression brightened at the prospect of capturing a new piece of the puzzle of her past. "Really?"

Connie nodded. "Absolutely. Your caustic sense of humor used to get Mildred and me in tons of trouble in high school. You would whisper something outrageous, we would start laughing—"

"Then *we* would get detention," Mildred finished.

"Sorry," Sam mumbled.

"Please don't you dare be sorry. We would have died of boredom if it hadn't been for you and Grace."

The name brought a sudden and complete halt to the tenuous sense of ease she'd felt during their last few minutes of conversation. Connie made a point of tracing the edge of the coffee table, her eyes averted. Mildred reacted similarly, moving away from Sam on the pretext of admiring an abstract painting hanging on the wall above the fireplace.

"Chase told me about Grace," Sam said gently, reminding herself that these people weren't insulated from their grief the way she was.

"Did he really?" Connie asked, but it was obvious the woman was on the verge of spilling her secrets.

"Don't start with that nonsense, Connie," Mildred pleaded.

Connie threw her hands up and grunted. "I think it's only fair for Sam to know the truth." There was just enough sparkle in Connie's eyes for Sam to know she was enjoying herself.

"The truth can wait." Mildred's green eyes narrowed into warning slits.

"No, it can't," Sam insisted as she got to her feet. Quickly, her heart pounding hard against her rib cage, she took a seat next to Connie. She desperately wanted to be let in on the secret. Ignoring the little warning voice inside her head predicting disaster, Sam urged the woman to continue.

Confidently, and over the fervent objections of Mildred, Connie began to speak. "What exactly has Chase told you?"

"He mentioned that two of our classmates had died. He was explaining to me why they wouldn't be at the reunion." Sam wondered why the last part of her explanation sounded so defensive.

"Did he tell you how they died?"

Sam nodded.

"Connie," Mildred pleaded, "I really don't think this is the time or the place for you to be laying all this on Sam. For heaven's sake, it's her first day back."

Connie ignored the other woman's protests and turned her face so that her round, dark eyes bore into Sam's. "Did he mention that aside from the fact that they had all attended Gillian High, there is one other common denominator?"

"No."

"You see," Connie began, a devilish light sparkling in her eyes, "over the last ten years, both of our dear, departed classmates had been horizontal with Chase."

Chapter Five

His kiss was her first conscious thought of the new day. Smiling at the memory, Sam rolled onto her side and read the bright red numbers of the clock radio on the nightstand—five thirty-five. Letting out a sigh, she momentarily considered trying to force herself back to sleep, but quickly dismissed the idea and threw back the bedspread.

Tiptoeing down the hallway, she tugged together the edges of her robe and slipped past the closed door where she guessed Chase must be fast asleep. Obviously, he's more adaptable to time changes, she thought as she rummaged through the cabinets for the coffee things.

As she waited for the coffee to brew, her hand went to the small key dangling from the chain around her neck. Pulling it free from her nightclothes, she rubbed its warm, polished surface between her thumb and forefinger. A smile curved the corners of her mouth as the smooth feel of the little metal key reminded her of

Karen. Turning, Sam looked out at the dark, unfamiliar landscape, decorated with cactus and an occasional jackrabbit. "This certainly is different from New York," she muttered softly. For a brief instant, she thought she saw a figure beyond the glass doors. "Don't start that again," she firmly instructed her imagination. "There's no one out there."

The sound of her voice echoed through the still house before being drowned out by sputtering steam as the coffee finished brewing. Still absently toying with the key, Sam used her free hand to pour coffee into a waiting mug.

As Sam cautiously took that first satisfying sip, she closed her eyes and thought about Connie's revelation regarding Chase and his past relationships with two deceased classmates of theirs. At the time, she'd been startled by the information; but after having thought about it half the night, she'd decided to just file that bit of information away until the time was right to question Chase about it.

It wasn't until she had seated herself at the round oak table that Sam felt the first stirrings of restlessness. No nurses or orderlies. "I'm alone," she said aloud. For the first time since the mugging, she was totally alone.

Her eyes followed the outline of the room to a point in the corner where a door stood closed. Sam wondered what was behind the door as she tapped her fingernail against the rim of her mug.

Sam's grip on her curiosity lasted through exactly three sips of coffee. She had to force herself not to slink like a criminal as she moved toward the closed door. *This is your house, Samantha. You have every right to open doors and look inside.*

It's probably just a closet, she told herself as she reached for the tarnished brass knob. The door creaked in protest as she tugged on it, gently at first, then with enough force to yank it free of the frame.

The interior was pitch-black. She felt along the inside wall until her fingers found a switch. Suddenly, the narrow, rectangular room was flooded with harsh yellow light from a naked bulb dangling from the ceiling. Sam squinted as her eyes adjusted.

The walls were lined with shelves that supported row upon row of dust-covered cardboard boxes. Ignoring the musty smell, Sam ventured a few steps into the cavernous closet and began to read the handwritten label on the end of one box.

"MJP 12/7/57-3/6/58."

The handwriting was vaguely familiar, but she knew it was not her own. Brushing away the top layer of dust, she began pulling down a similar box marked with the same initials, but with the dates being a three-and-a-half-month period in 1966. Sam heard a faint jingle as she tugged and pulled the box to the edge of the shelf. It was deceptively heavy, and she grunted in pain when the box came to rest on the top of her bare foot. Using her fingernail, Sam sliced through sealing tape, wrestled her fingers inside the top, then forced the box open.

Inside she discovered a neat row of what appeared to be cloth-covered books. The dozen or so volumes, labeled in the same neat hand, followed the time period chronologically. Tugging the first one free, she heard a tinkling sound as something dropped to the floor. Scanning the area around her feet, Sam couldn't locate the cause of the noise so she turned her full attention to the book.

She was surprised to find that it was held closed by a small brass lock. Since pushing the release button proved fruitless, she renewed her efforts to trace the object that had fallen when she'd pulled the book from the box. Her search was rewarded when she found a small collection of keys, nearly identical to the one around her neck, resting against the edge of one of the boxes on the floor.

She fit each key into the lock, and on the third attempt, she found the right key for the volume she held. With just a bit of urging, the tiny lock clicked, allowing her to press the button and release the flap of protective cloth from the front cover. The binding gave a stiff protest as she forced the book open. Inside she discovered neat columns of precisely written dates, followed by initials.

The last column of entries was actually decipherable. "Youngblood Home—Fairfield Clinic—No Further Contact," she read in a quiet voice.

It was obvious to Sam that the final entries were either the names of places or notations to the author. Whisking through the pages, she found each page contained similar entries. Replacing the first volume, she spent several minutes unlocking and inspecting the other books. It wasn't until the third diary that Sam's gray eyes stopped at an entry for November 19, 1966.

"PEH-married last Thursday."

What, she wondered, did all these entries mean? Her hand rose to the outline of the key at her throat. An alarming chill inched its way up her back. "Why would I have one of these keys with me in New York?" Her barren mind couldn't formulate an answer, and she felt a swell of angry frustration constrict her chest. "Could there be a connection?" she whispered in the musty confines surrounding her.

Tilting her head back, Sam scanned the shelves and found herself overwhelmed by the sheer quantity of boxes. If—and she knew it was a big if—the key they found near her on the night of the attack unlocked one of the hundreds of diaries stored in the closet, it could take her weeks to find the right one. And even then, she would have to find a way to decipher the strange entries.

Placing the book back in the box, Sam unclasped the chain from around her neck and placed the key in her palm along with the others. She noticed that it wasn't exactly like the ones she'd just found. The one Karen had given her was a bit larger and appeared newer than the ones from the box. "Maybe this is nothing more than a coincidence," she mumbled.

"What's a coincidence?"

Jumping at the sound of his voice, Sam let out a small cry when she painfully jammed her toe against the corner of something hard.

"Nothing," she said through clenched teeth. Turning, she found him silhouetted in the golden rays of morning. How long, she wondered, had she been rummaging in the closet?

"What are you doing in there?"

Scooting around the box, Sam sighed and moved toward the door. Chase angled his large frame to allow her to pass. The smell of coffee replaced the musty aroma of cloistered dust, and the air in the kitchen brought cooling relief to her warm skin.

She heard him close the door as she fussed with the edges of her robe. "I was just having a look around," she finally answered.

Out of the corner of one eye, she saw him shrug before moving over to pour himself a cup of coffee. Sam swallowed hard as she watched the crisp fabric of his pale green shirt strain against his muscled arms. Her tongue came out to dampen her suddenly dry lips, and she discreetly slipped the collection of keys into the pocket of her robe.

"Got any plans for the day?" he asked without turning to face her.

"Booked solid," she quipped.

"I've got to go out to my place. What to come along?" he asked, turning around.

"You have a place?" she asked. Then blushed furiously at the idiocy of her question. Holding up her hand, she said, "Of course you have a place—dumb question."

His lips curved into a lazy grin so innocently seductive that Sam felt her blush deepen.

"I need to go out there and check up on things."

"Where is 'there'?" Reading the momentary flash of disappointment in his dark eyes, Sam let out a sigh. "I'm sorry, I don't remember," she added.

"No big deal," he assured her with a forced lightness. "I have a small place at the edge of the reservation. Get dressed and we'll take a ride out there."

A HALF HOUR LATER she pawed through the clothes in her closet, plagued by indecision. Taking her lead from Chase, she finally decided on jeans and a silk blouse in a deep shade of royal blue. After a quick shower, she feathered the layers of hair around her face with nervous fingers. "Calm down, Samantha," she instructed her reflection. "It's just a drive, not a date, for heaven's sake."

Still, her heart pounded with more enthusiasm than she would have liked—especially when she remembered yesterday's kiss. She very nearly convinced herself that the extra minutes she spent primping in the bathroom were just to slow her racing pulse, which couldn't possibly have anything to do with the excited anticipation tingling in the pit of her stomach.

She began to relax shortly after they turned onto the flat ribbon of highway that appeared to go on into infinity. Chase flipped on the radio, filling the car with a twangy, male voice lamenting the loss of his beloved horse. Sam found herself smiling at the simplistic lyrics of the country tune.

"Now that's music," Chase said, tapping one booted toe to the beat as he reached to turn the volume a few notches louder.

"Is that what that is?" Sam asked in a saccharine voice.

His head swung around quickly, and the expression he wore was one of complete and utter surprise. "Before you went off to New York, you used to love country-western. It was the *only* kind of music you liked."

Concentrating on the song, Sam tried to rekindle some sort of enthusiasm for the whining wail about a felled stallion. It didn't happen. "It must be an acquired taste," she mumbled under her breath, trying not to cringe as yet another chorus began.

"What made you go exploring in Gran's closet this morning?"

"Those were my grandmother's things?"

Chase nodded and took one hand off the wheel to push back the brim of his Stetson. "As far as I know. I mean, that's what you told us when we were cleaning out the house after she died."

"When was that?"

"It's been almost a year and a half now."

"Did I ... did I come back here for the funeral?"

Chase shook his head. "Gran left strict instructions that there wasn't to be any funeral. Grace was the one you talked to. You made the decisions, and Grace took care of things at this end."

"That seems so cold."

Chase reached out and placed his warm hand over her knee, giving it a reassuring squeeze. "You did what Gran wanted. Believe me, she died beaming with pleasure over your success."

Sam's eyebrows crinkled pensively, hoping Chase was right and that she'd actually brought joy to someone.

She turned her attention to their surroundings. They had entered the mouth of a canyon, its eroded layers lined and flaky like a warm biscuit. "This place is breathtaking," she said, twisting in her seat in order to take in the panoramic view of auburn walls playing off the lime green cottonwoods that snaked their way along the banks of a small river at the bottom of the canyon.

"Welcome to *tsegi.*"

"Sssss ..." Sam tried in vain to repeat the unfamiliar word.

"It's a Navaho word that means 'rock canyon.' The Anglo name is Canyon de Chelly."

"It's gorgeous!"

"Unfortunately it's been turned into a tourist trap," he countered with a trace of bitterness.

"I can understand why. It's incredible."

After passing through the canyon, Sam found herself greeted by a weathered sign prohibiting hiking, camping and hunting.

"Welcome to the Navaho Nation," Chase announced, pride evident in his deep voice.

The quality of the paved road deteriorated almost immediately upon entering the boundary of the reservation. Sam gripped the shoulder belt in an effort to keep from being tossed around by the abundant potholes.

Chase turned at a sign that read Visitors' Center and stopped in front of the first building. It was an eight-sided wooden structure with an array of brightly colored, beaded dolls swaying from hooks around a large entrance. There was a plethora of hand-painted signs touting everything from the availability of photographs of authentic hogans to a sale on a six-pack of soda.

"This is where you live?"

"Hardly," Chase said with a chuckle. He flung open the door of the Land Rover and heaved his massive frame out onto the dusty surface below.

Sam followed his lead, curiosity moving her wide eyes in every possible direction. The smell of an open-air fire drifted over to them on the same breeze that carried the distant sound of children squealing in play.

"Samantha!"

Before she could react, she found herself wrapped in pudgy brown arms, her face smothered against an ample bosom.

"Let me look at you," the woman said, gently taking hold of Sam's upper arms and holding her at arm's length for an inspection. One hand reached up and smoothed a lock of hair from Sam's forehead. "You have not changed."

"You'll have to excuse my mother," Chase interjected. "She hugs first and saves the introductions for later."

"A respectful son does not correct his mother."

Sam's eyes darted between the two, instantly recognizing the similarities in their features.

"It's nice to see you," Sam said carefully.

"My poor dear," the woman cooed. "I am glad you are home where we can keep an eye on you. I always told Gran nothing good would come of your going to New York."

"It appears you were right," Sam agreed.

"The past is past," she said with a dismissive wave of her chubby hand.

"Please don't say it's best forgotten," Sam joked, feeling oddly at ease when she looked into the kind, dark eyes. "And don't you dare apologize!" she cautioned when she saw that the woman was on the verge of doing just that.

"Can we have some help here?"

Chase's mother turned in a huff, dragging Sam along with her as she went to attend to the couple standing just inside the door.

"Have you decided?"

"We'll take the one with the snakes and birds."

Sam watched Chase and his mother exchange the oddest expression just before she left them to write up the sale. Sam couldn't help but gape as she took in the sight of the colorful crafts and handiwork displayed inside the small shop. Jewelry, artifacts, healing herbs and flowers, blankets and a unique form of painting cluttered every usable inch of the room.

"This is incredible! What is it called?" she asked Chase after going close enough to one of the framed paintings to examine it more closely.

"Sand painting."

"It is!" she screeched in a high-pitched voice. "I can see the little grains of sand stuck to the background. They're beautiful. Who makes them?"

"My mother. Bunny Lawson is something of a renowned local artist. Her reputation brings in a lot of tourist dollars."

"And that bothers you," she surmised. It appeared to Sam that mother and son had what Dr. Masters called "unresolved issues."

"No, it doesn't," he assured her defensively as he drifted over to a nearby soda machine.

"Testy," she commented, turning her attention to a collection of turquoise jewelry encased behind smudged glass.

"Perhaps if my son had suffered your fate, he would make his choices more wisely," Bunny said as she scooted around the back of the counter so that they spoke to each other across the jewelry case.

"What choices are you speaking of?" she said.

"We will save that for another time. I want to know what I can do to help you."

"Thank you, Mrs. Lawson, but I can't—"

"Bunny, please. You have always called me Aunt Bunny, but I suppose you are old enough to drop the 'aunt.'"

"Bunny," Sam repeated slowly, testing the name on her brain. It was a fruitless experiment.

"Are you all right? You look a little flushed."

"Fine," she insisted with a smile. "It must be the heat."

"Chase!" Bunny bellowed. When he reappeared, Sam was relieved to see that the deep lines no longer marred the edges of his expressive eyes. "If you're taking Sam out to the house, I hope you had the good sense to bring along a hat for her."

"I . . . um." Chase scraped the worn wooden floor with the toe of one boot.

"Here." Bunny reached behind her and selected a hat from the rack behind the register. Placing it on Sam's head, she eyed her other choices for a moment, then took back the first hat and produced a second, smaller one.

"This will do."

The weight of the hat felt strange, and Sam was tempted to return it to her, but something told her that Bunny wouldn't take kindly to such an act of rebellion.

A few minutes later, after they left Bunny to deal with a sudden influx of camera-toting customers, Sam found herself grateful for Bunny's thoughtfulness. The hat kept the glare of the noonday sun from blinding her as they traversed the maze of roads.

"What have you done to irritate your mother so?"

"Did she tell you she was irritated?" Chase asked without looking in her direction.

"Not really. I just sensed a little bit of friction between the two of you."

"I probably forgot to take the trash out for her."

Sam didn't think his words rang true, but then, the only basis for her conclusion was instinct, and she wasn't exactly batting a thousand in that department. She might have pressed him further had they not, at that moment, turned off the main road onto a smoothly paved driveway lined by crude fencing.

The building at the end of the driveway was a modest ranch house, well cared for and landscaped with cacti and small red wildflowers. There were several outbuildings beyond the house, all enclosed within the line of fence that stretched as far as the eye could see.

The air coming in through the Land Rover's vent brought with it the unmistakable scent of animals nearby.

"This is where you live?" she asked.

"You got it on the first guess."

"Is this a farm?"

"Kind of. We breed horses."

"Horses? Really?" She couldn't keep the squeal of delight out of her voice, though she had no idea why such knowledge should fill her with ebullience.

"I thought you spent most of your time at Greenhaven studying. Didn't you learn all about the Indians and our long history of raising and training horses?"

"I'm afraid history wasn't my strong suit. I got about as far as Columbus sailing the ocean blue to discover America in 1492 and threw in the towel."

"If Columbus discovered America, what were we?"

"Sorry," Sam said after she realized what she had said.

"Don't apologize, Sam," he said, slipping his arm across her shoulder as he led her up the steps.

The interior was decorated much the same as the interior of his mother's shop. Everything looked handmade, warm and welcoming. The vision of her New York apartment flashed in her mind, and she couldn't stop the shudder that accompanied the thought.

"Is something wrong?" Chase queried, turning her gently so that they stood inches apart, his breath warming her face.

"No, I'm fine," Sam croaked out the lie and attempted to take an abrupt, awkward step away from him.

He released his hold on her long enough to remove first his hat, then her own. Tossing them onto a nearby chair, Chase gently coaxed her into his arms, until he could feel every supple curve of her against him. His head bent down closer, his mouth teasing hers with a feathery brush.

He felt her legs begin to weaken as a fierce, burning desire started in his stomach and released a rapid, molten fire into every vein in his body. This wasn't part of the plan, but he couldn't seem to help himself. Her enthusiasm for life—and everything around her—was rejuvenating and refreshingly honest.

Honest.

The word put an instant damper on the flame of his passion, and Chase moved away from her. He felt guilty when he saw the confused series of lines wrinkling her forehead.

"This isn't fair of me, Sam," he told her through a forced smile.

"I don't understand," she said.

"You will," he promised her, feeling as if his shoulders might buckle from their burden.

He thumbed through a stack of mail he'd gathered when they walked into the house. Sam wondered why he had kissed her—she also wondered when he might do it again.

"Want to come down to the pen? I have to tend to one of the horses, but it won't take me too long."

"Sure, I'll tag along, if I won't be in the way."

She followed Chase on the short walk to a corral just beyond the house. Sam climbed up on the top railing of smooth fence and watched as he methodically began washing, brushing and whatever else it was he was doing to a beautiful animal that was the grayish color of snow-laden clouds. Eventually, she turned her attention to an adjoining pen and watched as several wobbling baby horses struggled to keep pace with their sturdier parent. She tried to remember the word for a baby horse, but it just wouldn't come.

Chase moved on to tackle a few other chores, leaving Sam to enjoy her surroundings. She loved the feel of the sun against her skin almost as much as she enjoyed the feel of Chase's body against hers—almost.

"Stop it," she warned herself aloud. At the sound of her soft voice, the horse Chase had been working on sauntered over to her. Her initial fear quickly gave way to pure pleasure as she patted the animal's coarse hair and he offered his nose to her.

"How did you get a name like Justice?" she asked the horse. She'd heard Chase say the name over and over as he'd worked on him. "That's all right, you don't have to answer. At Greenhaven, a lot of the patients didn't talk. I'm sure that after a few weeks with Dr. Masters, you'd be talking up a storm."

"And what would I say?"

Sam swatted behind her, careful not to startle the animal in the process. "Very funny, Chase," she said.

"You're the one recommending overpriced therapy to a horse."

In one lithe movement, Chase hoisted himself up onto the railing next to her, the wood creaking in response to the added weight.

"This is a very nice place you have here," Sam said to break the uncomfortable silence that was daring her to reach out for him.

"We're getting there."

"We're?"

"My brother and I work together."

Sam got the distinct impression that he wanted to say something else. Whatever it was, he apparently decided to remain silent. He jumped down from the railing, grasping her from behind and effortlessly lifting her down. "You'd best get out of the sun. You can have a drink while I grab a quick shower. Then we can head back."

Chase took a different route back into town, showing her various sites along the way. Sam found herself becoming enthralled with Gillian, and she questioned him unendingly about the places they encountered.

"I'm a little hungry," she said. Shifting to sit sideways in the seat, Sam had a sudden and desperate desire to be part of a crowd. She still wasn't entirely used to her hard-won freedom. "Where can we get something to eat around here?" she asked.

"You've got two choices." His eyebrows arched at her shocked expression. "This isn't the big city. Hell, we don't even have carryout in Gillian."

"So what are my choices?"

"The Well, although I'm not sure you're quite ready for The Well yet. How about Rafe's?"

"Am I supposed to have an opinion?"

"It's a pretty decent place, great quesadillas."

Sam didn't dare ask what a quesadilla was, she figured she'd find out soon enough.

From the outside, it didn't appear that Rafe devoted much of his time to general maintenance. That may have been why Sam was so taken aback when she saw the interior of the restaurant. The walls were lined with intimate booths, while the center tables were decorated with festive pottery pitchers. The smell of hot, spicy food got her mouth watering even before the hostess offered her greeting.

"Afternoon, Chase, ma'am, table for—"

"Sam! Chase! Over here!"

They looked up to find Mildred frantically waving her pale, thin arms above her head.

"You folks go on and join them. I'll bring the extra settings."

Sam went first, weaving her way through the sparsely populated tables to where Mildred, Connie and an attractive light-haired man had risen, waiting to greet them.

"Samantha Parrish, this is my fiancé, Jack Gillian. Jack, this is Sam," Mildred said.

Sam smiled at the gracious blond man who had politely captured her hand in both of his. His smile was warm, and his light blue eyes glittered with pleasure.

"Mildred has told me so much about you. Your coming back for this reunion has been the perfect reward for all her hard work."

"Come on, Jack. No need to butter Sam up. I doubt she's even registered to vote in this state," Chase chided good-naturedly as he shook the man's hand.

"I'm counting on you to change her mind," Jack countered with a wink of his eye. "I'll need all the support I can get come November."

"You're a politician, Mr. Gillian?" Sam asked, only to realize her question brought about a round of smothered giggles from everyone but Chase.

"I'm a U.S. senator, Miss Parrish. I'm running for reelection."

"Sorry," she said tightly, wide-eyed with embarrassment. "I'm a bit out of touch with the identities of elected officials."

"I can imagine," Jack said in a tone that wasn't at all pitying. "I must say, it's quite a pleasure for me to meet you after all these years. When I first started dating Mildred, she insisted that we tape your show every day. I wouldn't want this to get around, but I'm still quite a fan of *Secret Splendor.*"

Sam laughed as she took the seat between Chase and Jack.

"All of us here in Gillian took some small measure of pride in your fame."

"Thank you, Mr. Gillian."

"Jack, please. Mr. Gillian makes me sound too much like my father and not enough like an individual."

Noting his expensive suit, good looks and charm, Sam found it hard to believe that the man had any trouble projecting his own unique personality. "Can I assume from your name that there is some connection?"

"My ancestors founded this town in 1882."

"Were you part of our class, Jack?" Sam asked. Her innocent remark inspired some well-intentioned ribbing from Mildred and Connie.

Connie leaned forward on her elbow as she spoke. "Jack went to boarding school. His daddy was probably afraid he'd end up marrying someone like Mildred if he stayed in Gillian."

"Stop it, Connie!" Mildred chided, nudging the dark-haired woman just hard enough to make her point.

The banter was hard for Sam to follow at times. And the fact that nearly every time someone made a comment, they would have to footnote it with an explanation for her benefit made things a bit uncomfortable. Chase usually managed to fill in some of the gaps, but the experience left her wondering if her decision to return to Gillian for the reunion was such a good idea, after all. After a little while, she excused herself and went in search of the ladies' room. The woman near the entrance directed her to a long corridor on the other side of the bar. The small cubical smelled of sickeningly sweet citrus, and Sam considered opening the window for air while she touched up her makeup. Her hand was near the sash when her attention was drawn to the parking area.

That's odd, she thought. She could have sworn she saw Chase standing along the side of the building, having an animated conversation with someone partially obscured in the shadows. They were too far for her to hear what they were saying, but judging from his body language, she didn't think Chase was too pleased with the topic.

His arms flailed, followed by some rather emphatic slapping of one hand against his open palm. At one point, he even removed his Stetson and whacked it against the stucco exterior of the building.

"I wish I could see who you were fighting with," Sam whispered. At the sound of the door opening, Sam jumped back to the sink, lowering her guilty eyes.

"We were afraid you'd gotten lost!" Mildred chided.

"It just takes me a while," Sam lied. "Jack seems very nice."

Mildred's reflection froze for just a fraction of a second before a perfect smile brightened her expression. "I'm a very lucky lady."

"When are you getting married?"

"This fall. After the election."

"This must be a chaotic time for you."

"Not me," Mildred assured Sam with a wave of her slender finger. "I like political life. I like most kinds of volunteer work. I'm well suited to it."

Not knowing what to say, Sam simply nodded.

"Speaking of which—" Mildred reached out and captured Sam's arm "—do you think you could spare a few hours to give me a hand with preparations for the reunion?"

"I don't know," Sam began, then quickly amended her response when she noted disappointment on the other woman's face. "I'd be happy to help you."

"Thanks, Sam. Shall we go back?"

Sam agreed but managed to catch a quick glimpse out the window before they left. Chase and his mysterious contact were nowhere to be seen.

She stopped short when they stepped into the dining area and Chase was just as she had left him. Even his hat occupied the same spot beneath his chair. "I'm losing it," Sam muttered.

"What have you lost?" Connie asked.

"Nothing. I was just thinking out loud," she said as they resumed their positions at the table.

"So what have you been doing to keep yourself occupied today?" Connie asked.

"We went out to my place," Chase answered. "Nothing special."

"Has your being home helped you with your memory?" Mildred asked.

"Not really," she answered with a shake of her head. "Nothing in the house seems familiar to me."

She leaned forward and spoke more softly. "I've actually taken to snooping through closets just to get my bearings."

"Don't push yourself," Jack cautioned.

"Don't worry, I'm keeping an eye on her," Chase announced.

"What kind of snooping?" Connie prodded.

Sam laughed. "It's my grandmother's stuff, so I'm told. I just found a closet full of diaries this morning."

"Diaries!" Connie exclaimed, rubbing her jeweled hands together in a devious manner.

"What kind of diaries?" Mildred asked.

"I don't have a clue," Sam admitted. "None of the entries make any sense to me, but I'll keep trying to decipher them."

"Just so you leave time to help me," Mildred cautioned.

"Don't worry," Sam promised with a smile. "Just tell me when and where, and I'll help with whatever needs to be done."

By the time they left the restaurant an hour or so later, Sam felt as if she'd just taken a crash course in political science.

She wanted to get Chase talking. She was hoping for the opportunity to ask him about the scene she'd witnessed in the parking lot. "I don't know much about politics, but Jack sounded like he had some good ideas."

Chase shrugged and let out a breath. "I'm sure he'll get reelected. Between his father's clout and his conservative position on most issues, he's a virtual shoo-in."

"Is that good, or bad?"

"Good, I suppose, but I'm always a little wary of intolerance."

"I don't understand."

"Jack gets a lot of support from radical, right-wing religious groups. I'm just not convinced that government is the proper place for radicals on either end of the political spectrum. It hinders compromise."

"Does that make you one of those 'mealymouthed moderates' Jack was talking about?"

Chase grinned and tipped his Stetson. "I believe it does."

"Compromise is nice," she said. "Speaking of which, I thought I saw you in the parking lot at Rafe's arguing with someone."

"What?" Chase asked in a surprised tone. "When would I have been in the parking lot?"

"It must have been someone that looked like you," Sam conceded, though she could have sworn the smudge of ecru paint on the brim of his hat was the same color paint that was on the building.

THE MESSAGE LIGHT on the answering machine was flashing when they entered her grandmother's house. Sam was trying to figure out which button to press when Chase reached around her, his hand brushing her skin, and pushed the proper button. The fact that he had unbuttoned his shirt and tugged it free from the waistband of his jeans didn't help her mechanical abilities in the least. Ignoring the path of warmth left in the wake of his touch, Sam listened as a familiar voice came over the tape.

"Hi, it's me, Karen. Call me as soon as you get in." A short beep followed, then another message from Karen, only this time her voice had an edge to it that inspired real concern in Sam.

"I don't want to alarm you, but I know something that I think might help you." There was a brief pause in the message, then Karen said, "I'm not going to be your replacement on *Secret Splendor*. I've made a terrible mistake, but I *didn't* know. Call me as soon as you can."

"I wonder what that's all about?"

"Why don't you call her and find out?" Chase suggested, his expression serious.

Rummaging through her purse, Sam found her address book and quickly looked up the number. Her finger trembled slightly as she pressed the numbers in careful succession.

"Hello."

"This is Samantha Parrish," she told the male voice. "May I speak to Karen, please?"

"Hold on."

"I'm sorry, Miss Parrish, but Miss Quinn isn't available. Can I ask the reason for your call?"

Sam covered the receiver with her palm. "There's some man on the line. He said Karen isn't available, and he wants to know why I'm calling."

Chase took the receiver from her. "Who is this?" he demanded without preamble.

"I see," he said, his face closing into a tightly guarded expression.

After what felt like hours, Sam could no longer bear his expression—or the silence as he listened solemnly to the speaker. "What?" Sam demanded, but got no reply.

"When was that?"

"When was what?" she demanded in a loud voice, which Chase chose to ignore by placing his hand against his free ear.

"Tell Detective Burns he can reach us here all evening."

Slowly, Chase replaced the receiver, his dark eyes scanning her face. "They found Karen about an hour ago. She's dead."

Chapter Six

"Dead?" The word came out in a tone as hollow as its meaning.

Chase nodded before pulling her into his arms. Her body shook with uncontrolled sobs, and he felt powerless to do anything to comfort her. Stroking her hair, he stared at the wall, trying to give himself some perspective.

"She can't be dead, Chase," Sam said between sobs. Her eyes were red and brimming with tears when she turned her face to his.

"I'm really sorry," he replied as she collapsed against him in grief.

Seeing her beautiful eyes filled with anguish and fear only made him feel more protective—and guilty.

"Sam, let me take you into the living room," he suggested as he steered her shaken form into the adjoining room. It was several long minutes before her sobs melted into tremors of raw emotion. He wondered where he could find the strength to continue the charade. Seeing her torn to pieces was too hard. He sat patting her shoulder with her head resting against his chest.

It wasn't the same as before and he knew it. The woman in his arms had an uncanny inner strength, yet he suspected that she was still emotionally fragile. The injuries had left her isolated. He also knew that Karen had played an important role in Sam's recovery. He'd seen the rapport between the two women. It was obvious that Sam had treasured her friendship with Karen. Karen's death left Sam with no one. No one but him, and he could only reach her from the bridge of his own deception.

"How could she be dead?" Sam asked when he appeared from the kitchen some time later with a cup of hot tea.

Chase's expression was pained. "Drink this."

"Thanks. Did the police say what happened?"

Gravely, he lowered himself next to her on the sofa. His dark eyes met and held hers. "There's time for this later. I think you ought to lie down."

"No!" she retorted quickly. "I don't want to be alone now."

He nodded and gathered her against him again. Sam listened to the sounds of his breathing as the tears continued to roll unchecked from her eyes. It was impossible to think of Karen as anything other than a vivacious, living being. How could she die? She asked Chase the same question.

"Accidents happen."

His statement seemed to open a new door in her mind. Sam had been so wrapped up in her sorrow that she had barely considered the means which had taken her friend from her. Placing her cup on the table, she reluctantly eased herself away from Chase.

"Accidents?"

"I'm sure it wasn't intentional."

Her comprehension was slow, but she eventually caught up to him. "Karen had an accident?"

"In a manner of speaking."

"Don't hedge, Chase. Tell me what the police told you."

"I think we should save—"

"I don't want to save anything." Her hand reached out and grasped his arm. She gave him a gentle squeeze. "I need to know what happened."

"It was an overdose."

"Overdose? As in drug overdose?"

"Yeah, but they won't know which drug until they get the results of the autopsy."

The image of her friend's body being dissected for autopsy turned Sam's stomach. Her voice grew louder, inspired by fierce indignation. "Karen was not into drugs. In fact, she was really helpful to me when I was weaning myself off painkillers after my attack."

Chase nodded, obviously content to let her get her feelings and frustrations out.

"I just don't believe that she would suddenly take up drugs. The last time she came to visit me at Greenhaven, Karen was ecstatic about the possibility of signing on permanently with *Secret Splendor*. And you saw her at my place only a couple of days ago. Karen certainly didn't seem suicidal at that point.''

"Nope," Chase agreed with a slight nod of his head. "But you heard the message she left. Maybe she couldn't handle the fact that she didn't get the part."

"Chase," Sam began in a clear voice that was no longer cracking from the shock, "Karen was a woman who treated life's little curveballs as challenges."

Sam's eyes narrowed, and she intently studied the man across from her for several minutes. His actions were supportive, but Sam had the distinct impression that his attention was somewhere else. Deep lines edged the corners of his eyes, and his mouth was curved in a very definite frown.

"Did you hear me?"

Chase averted his eyes and appeared to be on the verge of answering her question when the shrill ring of the telephone split through the air. He jumped up, patently ignoring the fact that it was her house, and raced to the phone.

"Lawson."

It was just as it was before, only this time, Chase showed her the common courtesy of covering the receiver and mouthing "Detective Burns" as he listened to the caller without bothering to fill her in on any details as he went along.

Exasperated, Sam blew a stream of air in the direction of her forehead and tried to convince herself that this was all some sort of bad dream—make that a nightmare, she amended. The frantic sound of Karen's recorded message nagged her like an unreachable itch. "What did she mean about making a mistake? And what was it she wanted to tell me so badly before she died?" she said aloud.

"Hold on a second," Chase said as he covered the receiver. "What did you say?"

Jolted by the sound of his voice breaking through her private thoughts, it took her a second or two to compose her response. "I was just wondering about the messages. Did you tell Detective Burns about her calls?"

Chase nodded and spoke into the phone in a hushed whisper.

The longer Chase stayed on the phone, whispering like some teenager making plans for a late-night escapade, the more anxious she felt. By the time he finally placed the receiver back on the hook, Sam's suspicious eyes had narrowed into militant slits.

"What's going on? I can almost hear your brain working from here," Chase said expectantly.

"It's the connection," she began tentatively. She wanted so much to share her thoughts, but she was terribly afraid that he would think she'd lost her mind.

"Between you and Karen?" he finished for her.

"C'mon, Chase. In the past two days, I've learned that three people I've known have died in accidents. Not to mention that I was beaten and left for dead."

Chase moved quickly, holding her against him. "I know it must be awful for you, but there's really no distinct connection."

"No connection?" she asked incredulously after she had pulled away from him. "There's me."

"Sam." His voice had a forced quality to it. "Don't let your imagination run wild."

"What if it is me?" she retorted. Rising, she hugged her body as she paced in front of the coffee table.

"How could it be you?" Chase reasoned.

"Friends of mine keep turning up dead? Wouldn't that bother you?"

"I'm not dead," he proffered reasonably.

So reasonably that Sam began to doubt her theory.

"There isn't a connection, Sam."

"I guess you're right," she relented. "I just didn't realize the effect of Burns's words on me. I wish he wouldn't have told me that there was a possibility my attacker might come back to finish the job. I suppose I've got to stop hunting for some grandiose conspiracy around every corner."

"Good idea," he said with a crooked smile that brought about a small one in return.

"I should probably call Karen's parents and find out where to send flowers."

"You don't want to go back to New York?" he asked, making her feel instantly guilty for her breach of etiquette.

Truth be told, Sam had no desire to see her friend laid out in a coffin. The image sent a shiver the full length of her spine. "If I go, my presence will only turn the whole thing into a sideshow. I'm not sure her family would appreciate that."

"I think you have to go, Sam," he insisted. "You told me yourself that Karen was always there for you."

"You're right," she admitted. "I'll call the family in the morning for details."

"Do you want to lie down for awhile?"

"You sound like you're in a hurry to get rid of me." She meant nothing by the remark, but Chase appeared crestfallen by it. "Maybe a long soak in the tub," she countered, glad to see the relief return some of the sparkle to his dark eyes.

A short while later, conflicting thoughts whirled inside her brain as steam from the bathwater swirled around her head. So much death. She remembered her conversation with Connie and Mildred and hated herself for the brief moment when she'd allowed her mind to question Chase. "I am being paranoid!" she chided. Chase could *not* have killed Karen. "He's not a killer, period."

CHASE STOOD in the backyard, absently grilling two steaks. He hoped the contact would come while Sam was still in the tub. She was getting suspicious, and he couldn't blame her. "They underestimated you, Sam," he said as he took a swallow from a bottle of beer. The liquid was cold and bitter, much like the way he was feeling about his predicament. He wanted out, and he'd told them as much. He couldn't go through with it. Not now. Not when he was dangerously close to losing his objectivity, thus his edge.

"She's the one that loses," he told a scampering lizard.

"Loses what?"

"You scared me!" he exclaimed, hoping to side-track her.

"Sorry."

Her hair was damp and mussed from her bath. The robe she had tied around her small waist forced him to take another long swallow of beer. It was pink silk. Soft pink silk. Off-limits pink silk. But for how long? he wondered.

"Can I ask you about something?"

"Shoot."

"Okay," she began, clearing away the sudden hoarseness in her voice. "The two classmates that died, is it true that you... that you and they..."

"If you're trying to ask me if I had relationships with Grace and Patty, the answer is yes."

"What about now?"

"Do you mean, am I involved with anyone now?" Sam nodded.

"No."

"Connie said yesterday that the only thing the two women had in common was their...um...involvement with you."

Chase threw back his head and laughed. The sound filled the early-evening air and went on for several seconds. A smile had found its way to her mouth by the time Chase turned his eyes to her.

"Connie's logic is interesting, but I can assure you, no one has ever died because they dated me."

Sam swallowed—hard. Her imagination kicked into overdrive as she tried to envision this man with the two women from the photographs. She could only muster a mental picture of herself with him. The vivid image in her brain brought an instant reddening to her cheeks, and her eyes flew open wide.

"Forget I asked you about that," she said weakly. "You have an uncanny ability to grasp situations—like with the car nearly running us down. It all seems easy for you."

"I'm just an observant person."

"I don't know," she hedged, absently playing with the key around her neck. "Maybe I'm not the connection between these accidents. But I'm having a hard time swallowing the fact that in the course of . . . how many months has it been?"

"Thirteen."

"In the course of thirteen months, three people have died, and I came about as close as you can get."

His back was to her when he spoke. "I think you're imagining—"

"Maybe I am imagining things," she interrupted. "But you could help me."

"Me?"

"You're very observant, you have a knack for picking up on details."

"I'm a horse breeder not a detective, Sam."

"I know, I just need your help."

"I don't think there's anything I can do for you."

Not willing to be brushed aside, Sam walked around and forced him to look her in the eye. "You can help me figure out if there's a connection."

"I told you there wasn't a connection." Chase jabbed at one of the steaks.

"For my own peace of mind?" she asked softly.

She watched the effect her words were having on him. She knew that his resistance was probably due to his apparent desire to shield her from anything negative. Sam was growing more and more attracted to that side of him. He attracted her physically, but she knew there was more to her feelings than that. His sensitive side came out in the way he had gently rocked her through those first harrowing hours of grief. That, plus the way he had supported her that first day at Greenhaven.

"Please?"

He closed his eyes and shook his head before a slight smile curved the corners of his mouth. "I'll help you in whatever way I can," he finally agreed.

"Thank you."

THEY BEGAN after breakfast the following morning. She pulled the mismatched keys from her robe pocket and said, "All right, Mr. Observant." She led him to the closet, tugged open the door and switched on the light. "Each one of these boxes holds diaries that contain weird entries. See if your observant self can make some sense out of any of them."

Chase was about to reach for a box when there was a knock at the front door.

"Mildred and Connie! I forgot they were coming by this morning," Sam said. "Could you please get the door, while I put this stuff away." Chase did as instructed while Sam closed the closet and returned the keys to their place in her robe pocket. She was winded by the time she joined the trio in the living room.

"You're not even ready," Mildred said with a frown.

"Ready for what?" Chase asked.

"We're taking Sam shopping today. She needs something dazzling for the reunion tomorrow night, and Connie and I have already found the perfect dress in a small shop over in Midgville."

"You didn't tell me about any shopping trip," he said to Sam, his eyebrows knitted together.

"I forgot," she admitted.

"Do you still want to go?" he asked.

"I'd better. I promised Mildred I would help her write out name tags afterward."

"If you don't feel—"

"Chase," Connie interrupted. "We're taking her shopping, not to a foreign country."

He shifted and there was a slight contraction of the muscles in his upper arms. "I know that, but yesterday—"

"I forgot to tell him," Sam inserted. Chase looked at her quizzically but didn't tell the two women about her recent loss. "Go get yourselves some coffee while I get dressed. I won't be long." She didn't feel much like shopping, but this was a chance to do some of her own investigating.

"YOU BETTER BE CAREFUL, Samantha," Connie warned as she unlocked the car. "I've always believed that the reason Chase never married was because of you. The man just could never get you out of his system."

"Even after you left for New York," Mildred added.

"I thought he went into the army the summer after graduation," Sam said.

"He did," Connie confirmed. "But he expected you to be waiting for him, here in Gillian, when he got out."

"Did I say I would?" she asked softly.

"Heavens, no!" Connie exclaimed. "You always told us that you were going to be a star and that then your father would—"

"Connie, can't you keep your foot out of your mouth for just one day?" Mildred groaned.

"My father would what?" Sam asked, ignoring the bickering she now recognized was an important part of the relationship between her two companions.

"Your father would come forward and then...well, then you'd know who he was," Connie answered.

"Wow," Sam said breathlessly. "Was I really that fixated on finding out who my father was? I mean, why didn't my grandmother tell me?"

"Gran didn't know. No one did. And since your mom died when you were so small, there was just no way for you to find out," Connie said. "Especially since the only person who might know his identity wouldn't tell if her life depended on it."

"And who is that?"

"Bunny Lawson. She was your mom's closest friend."

"I think you've said quite enough, Connie. This is supposed to be a fun outing, not your personal platform for spreading rumor and innuendo."

"But," Connie continued, ignoring Mildred and turning in her seat so that she faced Sam who was in the back seat of the expensive car, "over time I've heard folks speculate that your daddy was definitely from Gillian. Your mother never took any trips or anything, so she never had an opportunity to hook up with anybody."

Sam's laugh was without merriment. "Well, now I suppose it's a moot point. I wouldn't know my own father if I tripped over him. Funny how life doles out its own little ironies."

"Anyway," Connie continued, "Chase never wanted you to go to New York. I guess somehow he knew, as we all did, that once you got your break, you'd never be back."

"Yet here I sit," Sam countered.

"How long are you planning on staying?" Mildred asked.

"I don't really know." Sam reached up and pushed her bangs away from her forehead; then remembering about her scar, she quickly returned them to their proper place. "There's nothing appealing to me about returning to New York. Gran's house is so much more inviting than my apartment. Not to mention the years of diaries I've made it my personal mission to decipher. I don't understand the entries, but I'm determined to figure out what they're all about before I leave Gillian."

"Well, do take your time about it," Connie said. "I love having you back. And I'm sure Chase is thrilled to have you within arm's reach again."

"What was so special about me and Chase?" Sam asked, hoping to fill in some of the gaps in her life. "You seem to forget that I have absolutely no memory of him, or little else, for that matter."

"Then it will be like starting over," Mildred insisted. "How absolutely romantic."

Connie pretended to stick her finger down her throat. "You'll have to excuse Miss Hearts and Flowers, she's just feeling like the Queen of Romance, what with marrying the crown prince of Gillian."

SAM WAS TREATED to an almost unending flow of information about herself. Connie proved to be a wonderful source of knowledge and the more forthcoming of her two companions.

"I'm the smart one," Connie whispered loud enough for Mildred to hear. "I didn't get sucked in to being on the reunion committee. But you girls have fun!" Connie said snidely as she dropped Sam and Mildred off in front of Gillian High.

"I left my car here so I can run you home when we're through," Mildred stated.

"Fine," Sam said, though most of her attention was riveted on the large building. They passed a guard's desk, but no one appeared to be manning it on this warm summer afternoon.

"We can work in the office. Mary isn't in today, but I'm sure you'll see her at the reunion."

"Fine," Sam repeated. Whoever Mary was seemed far less interesting than the photographs lining the painted cinder-block walls. Judging by the age and quality of the pictures, Sam decided they must depict the school's entire history.

"This way," Mildred instructed, leading Sam down a darkened hallway to a door marked Office. She unlocked the door and said, "You make yourself comfortable while I run down to the supply closet."

The room contained four vacant metal desks and that was it. Sam soon grew bored of watching the wall clock tick off the minutes. Five minutes later, she decided to venture into the hallway to take another look at the school's memorabilia. Maybe it would trigger something in her mind.

After exiting the room, Sam thought the corridor was even darker than before. A tiny flicker of apprehension slowed her pace, but not her determination. She felt driven to search for some link to her past.

The pictures weren't marked with years, nor were they in any particular order. Sam found the activity educational, but very frustrating. When the sound of a door closing reached her ears, Sam turned in the direction of the noise.

At the far end of the hall stood a figure dressed all in black. Remembering the travesty in the airport garage, Sam yelled down the corridor, "Hi!"

The figure didn't respond verbally, but he did begin a slow, purposeful walk in her direction. Quelling her body's tremulous response, Sam yelled a second greeting.

His only response was to quicken his pace. Fear propelled her into action. Spinning on her heel, she immediately realized that the only exit was blocked by the dark figure. Since she couldn't get to the exit, she blindly began to jog down the corridor. Perhaps she could climb out a classroom window. Gillian High was on a fairly well-traveled road. All she had to do was get to the street.

Grabbing the knob on the first door, Sam let out a little cry when she found the door locked. Bracing herself, she made one futile attempt at jarring the door with her shoulder. "Ouch!" she groaned when her body contacted the heavy wooden door. The man was almost to the office, still moving an an annoyingly slow fashion that had her pulse and mind racing furiously.

There were no options except for her to try the doors. One by one, weaving from side to side, she twisted each knob in turn. She was making no progress, and he was closing in.

"Stay away from me!" she yelled over her shoulder. Her words did nothing to stop the squeak of his rubber soles as he continued his forward strides.

She was about to give up when to her utter shock and disbelief, the last door opened. The interior was pitch-black, and Sam had no idea where she was. All she knew was that she had to keep moving. She closed the door behind her and began feeling her way along the interior wall. For some reason her eyes refused to adjust to the darkness.

"*Ugh,*" she grunted when she felt something sharp rip through her slacks, puncturing the skin just above her hip. She hesitated, trying to feel the outline of whatever had caused her wound, when she heard the door open.

Sucking in her breath, she listened. He was in the room with her, she could feel the vibration of his feet hitting the floor. She remained perfectly still except for her hand. There were metal bars, spaced about a foot apart, with something wooden along the front. Careful not to make a sound, Sam slipped her perspiration-soaked body through the narrow opening.

Her eyes were finally beginning to adapt. She was inside a set of bleachers that had been collapsed like an accordion. Her hip hurt, and she could feel a small trickle of blood dampen her clothes. She didn't see him until they were close enough to touch one another.

His gloved hand skimmed the crack she was using as a porthole. Sam swallowed her scream and forced herself to remain perfectly rigid. She knew any sound or motion would give her away.

He stopped. Sam braced herself for discovery. She had been holding her breath for so long that her chest began to burn painfully. He had just begun to turn in her direction when the building filled with the blare of sirens. He turned and quickly left the room the same way he had entered.

Sam slowly let out her breath. She found that she was trembling, badly; and even though she was concerned about the significance of the screeching sirens, she stood for several minutes, trying to pull herself together.

"Sam? Are you in there?"

Sam quickly extracted herself from the bleachers, raced out of the room and ran directly into Chase's solid form. Mildred was with him and their expressions registered shock. Looking down, she saw the small stain of blood and wondered how she was going to explain what had just transpired.

"Oh, Samantha! First the mugging and now this," Mildred cried.

Sam looked up at Chase, suddenly wishing she had the nerve to ask him to hold her. "You aren't going to believe this," she began over the sirens, but then stopped abruptly when Mildred's comment sunk in.

"What do you mean, first the mugging and now this?" she asked Mildred.

"The sirens," she explained as she moved forward so that she stood between Sam and Chase. She took both of Sam's hands into her own and said, "The sirens... Samantha, your grandmother's house is on fire."

Chapter Seven

Chase's jacket was draped across her shoulders as Sam stood shivering from shock in the glow of the towering flames. Water from three separate engines arched into the fire, battling down the amber sparks. The heated air, thick with soot and the stench of various materials incinerating, did little to fend off the chill that permeated her as she watched the fire engulf a large portion of the house.

The area was buzzing with activity. Aside from the fire trucks, there were police cars and emergency vehicles lining the quiet streets, along with neighbors and a variety of other curious spectators. Scanning the scene, Sam's eyes searched for Chase, as she silently prayed he would reappear. It was odd that in such a short time she had come to depend on his strength and support. He made her feel safe, secure and special. He also made her feel like a woman, something she hadn't even known she'd missed.

Her legs were tired, and her hip was growing sore where she had injured it on the bleachers. Fear renewed itself as she recalled the incident at the school. "I know he was after me," she whispered. *The problem is how will I convince anyone else of that fact without having them think I've gone completely mad?*

HE WAS MAD. Chase couldn't believe the sight before him.

"How the hell could this happen?" the figure to his left demanded.

"Whoever it was must have seen me leave," Chase surmised.

The man shifted beneath the fire fighter's outfit he'd donned just in case anyone thought to question his presence at the scene. "We've got to be more careful. If she gets an inkling of what's going on, more than a year of work goes down the tubes."

"I know. I know."

"What's the problem?"

Chase shoved his fists into his pockets before answering. "I think she's beginning to suspect."

"Why do you think that?"

He shrugged, careful not to level a look in his companion's direction. He wasn't as afraid of Sam seeing this clandestine meeting so much as he was afraid of losing his temper. "She's getting suspicious because of the recent events in New York."

"Unfortunate, but we just have to proceed with the plan."

"I'd like to renew—"

"Your objections are on record, Lawson. You have your instructions." He turned and left with barely a sound.

Instructions. He repeated the word in his mind as he watched the firemen battle back the last vestiges of the fire. Turning, he spotted her sitting on the fender of one of the police cars. Her face was blank, as if she couldn't comprehend the destruction around her. Chase whispered a few expletives as he began the long walk to where he'd abandoned her when his contact had unexpectedly appeared.

"Why don't we sit in my car," he suggested gently.

With a zombie-like nod, Sam stood and he led her away from the partition of emergency-response vehicles. A faint layer of ash covered the Land Rover. Chase started the engine long enough to use the wipers to clear a visual path.

"Are you okay?" he asked quietly.

Sam turned to him, peering up through the thick veil of her lashes. He felt his chest grab and constrict.

"I'm fine," she answered.

"I don't know what happened," he began. "I left just after you did, and I know I didn't leave any of the appliances on, or anything."

She offered him a halfhearted smile before speaking. "I'm sure it's just an unfortunate accident."

Accident. The word seemed to plague her like some horrible recurrent nightmare.

"It doesn't look like the house is destroyed."

"No. The fire department seems to have saved the day."

The towering flames had ebbed, leaving only an occasional plume of curling smoke in their wake. The smell was the worst thing, she decided.

"I thought I'd take you back to my place," Chase said.

"Thanks." Sam was all too willing to accept a change of venue. Maybe if she stayed at his house, the "accidents" would cease.

"HE FOUND ME at the airport and the school," she mumbled.

"He who?"

They were headed toward the reservation, and Sam tried to pull her fragmented thoughts into a moderately cohesive explanation. Even in her own mind, the event she was going to detail seemed farfetched, bordering on paranoid. Chancing a look in his direction, Sam gathered her courage to speak from the strength in his profile and the kindness in his eyes. Her heart seemed to expand within her chest each time she looked at him. But right now, Sam didn't want to stop and analyze her thoughts or feelings—not when so many other areas of her life demanded closer scrutiny.

"I saw him again."

"Who?"

Sam marveled at his calm manner and casual tone. She watched him adjust his hat so that the brim shrouded his eyes.

"A man was following me at the high school."

"The guard?" he suggested.

"It wasn't the guard," she told him firmly. "And it wasn't a mistake in judgment, or my imagination, or the result of Burns's suggestion. He was after me, and I know he was going to hurt me."

She wasn't sure what she had expected, but it wasn't the pensive array of lines around his mouth. Something about his reaction bothered Sam, but she couldn't put a finger on any reason for her misgivings.

"Are you sure you weren't just—"

"I know what happened," she interrupted. "This man was calmly and calculatingly stalking me through the corridor. If I hadn't hidden in the bleachers, I'm absolutely certain he would have harmed me in some way."

After a few seconds, Chase reached out and gently patted her hands where they rested in her lap. The feel of his big, callused fingers gently stroking her brought a lump of emotion to her throat. "I need you to believe me, Chase!"

"I do," he said softly.

Sam let out the breath she didn't realize she'd been holding. "I imagine he's the same man who attacked me in Central Park."

"Did you recognize something about him?"

"No," she assured him, repeating Dr. Masters's organic theory about her failure to ever remember anything about the mugging. "I know I didn't make any enemies at Greenhaven. Unless you count the time I took Mrs. Findlay's checkers away because she was eating them."

"Where do checkers fall in the food pyramid?"

She laughed. "Fiber," she speculated wryly. Twisting in the seat, Sam was glad he wasn't able to see her expression. She felt sure her budding feelings for him would be evident in her eyes. She felt as if she belonged to him—as if being with him had somehow made her whole.

"Let's say it is the same guy," Chase began.

That thought immediately doused any pleasant thoughts she might have been imagining. "But why would he wait until now?" she pondered aloud. "It seems to me that he would have had several opportunities over the past year to finish what he had started."

"Maybe he didn't think you'd ever leave the sanatorium."

"I guess," she said with a sigh. "But that still doesn't help us find the connection between all these so-called accidents. It also doesn't explain why he torched my grandmother's house."

"Why do you think he's responsible for the fire?"

Sam gaped at him from the passenger's seat. "It's a little *too* coincidental, Chase." Why, she wondered, did he insist on playing devil's advocate at every turn?

"Let's say, for the sake of argument, that the deaths and your mugging are all related. That still doesn't mean the same person set the fire. Hell, Sam, we don't even know if the fire was intentionally set."

"I'm certain they'll find evidence that it was," she insisted.

"Okay," he said as he lifted his hand and stroked his chin. "What would he have gained by burning down the house?"

Pressing herself against the backrest, Sam considered the options. "Maybe he figures that I'll go back to New York if I don't have anyplace to live."

"Aren't you going back to New York, anyway?"

His voice had a slight edge that Sam hoped meant he wasn't in any great hurry to get her out of his life.

"I'm not sure what I'm going to do," she hedged. Closing her eyes, she waited, willing him to say something that would indicate that he shared some of her growing affection.

"What advantage would he gain if you went back? Your apartment is in a high-security building."

"So I'm more accessible here than I am in New York."

"That being the case, don't you think it unlikely the fire is connected to the deaths and your mugging?"

Sam found herself nodding. "Maybe the fire isn't, but I know in my heart that everything else is."

A few minutes later, they reached Chase's house. As he let her inside and into the kitchen, Sam kept a tight hold on the edges of his jacket. It wasn't until she saw her reflection in the toaster and turned to look at Chase that she realized just how ghastly they looked.

Their clothing was smeared with soot and grime. But it was the layer of ash and the odor of smoke clinging to them that made her feel excessively filthy. It was so bad that she refused the seat offered her by Chase.

"I'm afraid if I sit on that chair, it will reek of smoke for months to come."

"Good point," he agreed. "Let me fix you up in the guest room so you can get cleaned up."

"Thank you," Sam answered. She suddenly felt completely drained. As she followed Chase's broad shoulders, her legs felt as if they were weighted with lead. At least her hip no longer ached.

Chase ushered her into a small room that seemed to have its origins in the previous century. Rustic furniture was accented with colorful trinkets and artifacts. It was a warm, comfortable room, and she sensed that Bunny had had a hand in pulling it all together.

"The bath is through there," he said pointing to one of two doors. "I'll rummage through my closet and find something for you to put on."

Sam smiled. "Try for something you shrunk in the dryer," she said wryly.

"Right," he agreed, rubbing his large hands together as he left the room.

She could hear him in the next room and instead of feeling comforted by his proximity, a completely different feeling washed over her. She couldn't get her mind off him. Visions of Chase occupied most of her thoughts. Remembering the way he looked bared to the waist and perched on her bathroom sink brought a distinct warmth to the blood rushing through her veins. Those masculine shoulders, the flat, rippling muscles of his stomach—it was almost too much.

"Will these do?"

"What?" Sam asked hoarsely, hoping the soot on her face hid the warm stain spreading across her cheeks.

"These clothes?" he repeated, a look of concern creasing his forehead as his eyes roamed over her face. "Is something wrong?"

"Not a thing," she assured him as she grabbed the pile of neatly folded clothes and backed her guilty, blushing form toward the bathroom.

"Call if you need anything," he told her as he flashed that incredibly sexy grin.

"I will," she managed to call to his retreating back.

After removing her grimy clothes and placing them in a corner, she filled the tub and submerged herself in the soothing water.

As she lay there soaking, Sam thought about her life since the mugging and wondered if she would ever regain her memory. She thought about the two latest "accidents." First her friend, now her grandmother's house. Bit by bit, the links to her past seemed to be disappearing.

CHASE HAD GIVEN HER an old pair of sweats and a shirt she could have wrapped around her a second time. Toweling her damp hair, Sam grabbed the belt from her own slacks and secured her makeshift outfit as best she could. "At least my hip injury isn't serious," she told her reflection.

As she started toward the kitchen, she heard the muffled sound of Chase's distinctive voice and stopped just shy of the doorway.

"...I can't do it, O'Malley. I'm telling you, she's already spooked."

Who was O'Malley? Sam wondered as she flattened herself against the doorjamb. In doing so, she accidentally dislodged a small painting, which fell with a loud clattering to the floor.

"I've got to go."

She heard him replace the receiver in the cradle.

"Samantha?"

"Sorry," she yelled in to him. "I must have caught your shirt on the corner of the frame. I hope I didn't damage it."

"Not a problem," he said. His tone had a lingering hardness that only served to pique her curiosity.

She joined him in the kitchen, grateful for the mug of hot tea he had thoughtfully prepared. His hair was damp and small drops of water streaked down the front of his open shirt. She swallowed. The sight of his bronzed chest was almost more than her racing pulse could stand. She needed a diversion.

"Who's O'Malley?" she asked, careful to make the inquiry sound conversational.

"I don't know," he answered as he turned his back and began to survey the contents of his freezer.

"I thought I heard you say his name before I rearranged your wall."

"You must have misunderstood," he said dismissively.

Sam shook her head, certain of what she had heard. "You were talking on the phone," she prompted. "You told this O'Malley person that you weren't going to do something and that she was really spooked."

"No, Sam. I was talking to one of my buyers. We were discussing a horse. You probably overheard me say 'Oh, really,' as in 'Oh, really? She's really spooked?' "

Lowering her eyes, she studied the steam as she silently berated herself for eavesdropping and then misquoting him to boot.

"Were you thinking of calling the Quinns?" Chase asked, breaking into her thoughts.

Sam felt a pang of grief and nodded. Moving over to the kitchen phone, she grabbed a pad and pen and dialed New York Information. She wrote down the computer-generated number on the pad, then hung up and redialed.

Mr. Quinn answered and tearfully gave her all the details for the funeral. As he spoke, Sam wrote the name "Karen" over and over on the pad. After promising that she and Chase would be there for the service, Sam broke the connection.

Chase was staring at her, his eyebrows drawn together in a definite frown. "What is that?" he suddenly asked in a voice loud with excitement.

"Doodling," she said. "I was talking to Karen's father about—"

"Do you always do that?" His tone and volume gave her a start.

"Do what?"

"Doodle when you're on the phone?"

Sucking in a breath, Sam said, "I suppose I do."

"Did you do it before the mugging?"

"I wouldn't know," she reminded him gently.

"I can't believe it's as simple as your writing the same word over and over."

"Would you please slow down and tell me what has you all fired up?" Sam placed her hand on his forearm as she met his sparkling eyes with her own.

"It's probably nothing," he said, breaking the eye contact.

Sam was not ready to accept his apparent self-doubt. "Is this important?" she asked, waving the pad in front of him like the red flag of challenge.

His expression closed somewhat, but she noted just the slightest quiver in the determined set of his handsome chin.

"Tell me, Chase. I want to know." She moved her hand so that it rested against the bare skin near his stomach. She could feel the taut muscle beneath react to the contact. "Please?"

"The night you were mugged, when the cops searched your house, they found a notepad with one word written over and over again on it."

"What was the word?"

"Gillian."

Chapter Eight

"Why did I buy this dress?" Sam asked herself as she made a third attempt at fastening the row of tiny pearl buttons at the nape of her neck. Her arms were aching by the time she finally achieved success.

Glancing in the mirror, she decided the struggle was worth the effort. The deep blue dress was the perfect complement to her shape. Applying a dab of perfume to her wrists, she smiled in satisfaction at her reflection. "No one can accuse you of being showy," she said as she slipped on a pair of new pumps. Connie and Mildred had been right. The overall effect was understated, but perfect.

As she added a few last minute touches to her make-up, she tossed around in her mind the latest piece of the puzzle—Gillian. Why would she write that, over and over again, on a notepad? And was she referring to the town? the senator? or something else altogether? Unless she regained her memory, they might never know. One thing she did know: thinking about it was giving her a headache; and as she glanced at her watch, she realized she'd have to put it out of her mind—for now, anyway.

Her breath caught in her throat when she got her first sight of Chase where he stood waiting for her in the living room. Dressed in a gray, nubby, raw silk suit, with matching Stetson and boots, he looked like every woman's fantasy.

"You look great," he said in a tone that left no doubt in her mind that the compliment was genuine. "All set?"

Sam merely nodded, afraid she, too, would give away more with her tone than she dared.

Thanks to a quick shopping trip for toiletry items and such and the fact that she'd had the store deliver her outfit, she had been able to ready herself for the reunion with little inconvenience. *Except for the fact that I can't seem to keep my libido in check,* she added as Chase escorted her from the house.

It wasn't long before their destination, a brightly lit hall adjacent to the lone municipal building, came into view. The sign out front, which Chase informed her normally carried a public service announcement, welcomed the returning members of their high school class in big, block letters.

Chase pulled into a spot between two dusty pickups. The muffled sounds of boisterous conversations and loud music filled the gravel parking lot. Sam clutched the tightness at her midsection, trying to digest her nervousness. Was she anxious because she would be seeing so many friends who were now strangers? Or was it because of her being with Chase?

Though his face was shadowed by the twilight and the brim of a pale-colored Stetson, Sam watched as Chase sauntered ahead of her through the parking lot. *"Whew,"* she said softly as she watched him. Luckily, the sound of a car pulling into the lot spewing gravel muffled the remark. Chase, dressed for the occasion, was definitely a sight to behold—all broad shoulders, trim hips and angled features.

As her eyes ran down the back of his jacket, she found herself silently admiring her escort's perfect physique. Abruptly, he stopped just in front of the door, turned and placed a small kiss on her cheek. Her heart skipped a beat at the contact, and she instinctively placed her palms against his chest. Big mistake—her fingers rested against his solid mass, flooding her consciousness with sensation.

"What was that for?" she asked with a smile as she ran her hands over the lapel of his jacket. Her pale eyebrows arched teasingly, and she peered up at him through her lashes.

He smiled at her, treating her to a fabulous display of even, white teeth set against richly colored skin. His dark eyes twinkled mischievously, narrowing slightly as his vision traced a path to the swell of her breasts straining against the fabric of her dress. Wrapping his fingers gently around her upper arm, Chase steered her in the direction of the building. "Who would have thought you'd end up the success story of Gillian High?'' he said.

Sam felt a warmth rising on her cheeks. "I'm hardly the success story. I'm the *former* success who currently has brain damage and is dysfunctional."

"There's nothing wrong with your brain, Sam," he said, then bent lower so that his breath was against her ear. "And there's nothing wrong with the rest of you, either."

"Thank you. But I'm fairly certain I'll be the only woman in the room tonight who doesn't recognize a single individual."

"But they won't look as terrific as you do," he said softly. As he reached around with his free hand to grasp the shiny metal door handle, Sam thought about how grateful she was for this little respite from the confusion of her life. Tonight she vowed to abandon her sorrow and enjoy the festivities—and her companion.

She spent the next hour reacquainting herself with people. For the most part, they kept their curiosity at bay, though a few were rude enough to ask for all the gory details of the mugging. Friends she hadn't seen for ten years were strangers whom she found she enjoyed meeting. Her eyes periodically scanned the decorated room, searching for the three people whom she knew—Mildred, Connie or Chase. Disappointment wrinkled her forehead when she failed to find any of them among those gathered in small clusters partaking in animated conversation. "Blast," she muttered as she read the clock above the bar.

"Break a nail?"

Startled by the feel of his breath against her bare shoulder, Sam swatted playfully at Chase. Moving in front of her, he took a swallow from the long-necked bottle of beer gripped between his finger and thumb.

"Have you seen Connie or Mildred?"

Chase's lopsided grin widened at her question. "Nope, but I'm sure Mildred will be here soon. Her fiancé wouldn't pass up a handshaking opportunity like this."

"So she's going to marry an honest-to-goodness United States senator."

Chase nodded. "She'll get him reelected, too. Mildred lives for that man."

"I think that's wonderful!" Sam said after a moment of consideration. "Mildred deserves to be happy. She seems like a nice, down-to-earth sort of person."

One dark eyebrow shot up. "Mildred? Our Mildred? The girl who got a brand-new car for her sixteenth birthday, who had a fistful of credit cards as a teenager and who has never worn the same outfit twice?"

Chase stared down at her when she laughed. The action brought life to her large gray eyes, making them glint with genuine amusement. With her hair feathered short and framing her face, she looked much as he'd imagined she would—young and beautiful. When she was distracted by a classmate gushing compliments, Chase seized the opportunity and allowed his eyes to linger on the delicate curves of her slender body. The dress alone gave him more to think about than he would have liked. From the front it was rather simple, dark blue and beaded. But when she turned around, Chase was treated to an unobstructed view of her bare shoulders and back. The display of flawless, creamy skin was so inviting that he experienced a strong urge to reach out and stroke the furrow of her spine. Instead, he settled for another swallow of beer.

"...good to see you, too," Sam said, smiling. As soon as the couple was out of earshot, she rose on tiptoe and said to Chase, "Who were they?"

"You got me," he admitted.

"Maybe they weren't even our classmates. Maybe they saw all the cars in the lot and figured things were hopping at the community center."

As she started to lower herself, Sam lost her balance slightly. Reaching out, her hand made contact with Chase's solid forearm.

"Have you had a few too many?" he teased.

"I haven't had any," she retorted, feigning indignation.

"We could go out to my car and remedy that."

"Uhg!" Sam said with a look of mock disgust on her face—though a secret part of her experienced just the tiniest flutter of excitement. "I see it only takes you a few beers before the propositions start flying. Stop joking around and see if you can get the bartender to give me a soda."

Chase shrugged and grinned at her. His eyes, which were very nearly as black as the thick lashes surrounding them, met and held hers. "That's been your problem lately, Sam. You seem to have the mistaken notion that I'm joking."

"Oh, come off it!" she scoffed. "According to Mildred and Connie, your claim to fame in this lifetime will be that you scored more times in your senior year than the basketball team. And don't you dare deny it!" she added reproachfully.

Chase laughed at the motherly finger she shook in front of his slightly crooked nose. "I knew I should never have let you go off with that pair." Then he turned, wrangled a soda from the bartender and handed it to Sam.

His words sent a pleasant shiver through her. Sam found the response to his teasing more than just a bit exhilarating. Why did her body react to him so strongly?

"Why? Just because they warned me about the legendary conquests of Chase Lawson in his early years? Actually, they brought me up to the present. Save for a few years when you weren't in Gillian, and they couldn't keep tabs on your love life."

"Did they tell you that I once cared very deeply for you?"

"Let's change the subject," Sam suggested, lowering her eyes and placing her empty glass on the bar. "Besides, the way I heard it, you weren't *really* interested in me."

"Who told you that? You had great legs!"

"*Me*, Lawson, not my legs. Even in my immature teen years, I'm sure I understood the difference. Connie said the only interest you ever showed in me before our senior year was your expressed desire to slip your hands under my sweater."

"Connie talks too much," Chase said as he took another pull on his beer bottle. "Besides, the sweater thing was just one night when I'd had a bit too much to drink, and I spoke out of turn."

"So now you're telling me Connie was mistaken? What exactly were you trying to do that night?"

"Trying to get my hands inside your sweater," he admitted sheepishly. "Okay," he said, raising his arms in mock surrender, "I'll admit that my only motive that night was to convince you to join me in the back of my truck."

"Thank you for at least being truthful," Sam said with a roll of her eyes and sudden heat in her cheeks.

"And Sam," he said softly as his hand reached out to tilt her face toward his, "I want you to know the offer is still open." Leaning toward her, he gave her an exaggerated wink as punctuation.

"You are incorrigible!" she said with mock indignation and slapped his hand away from her face.

"But just think…if you slept with me now, I could sell the story to one of those cheap tabloids. You know, 'My Night of Passion with Samantha Parrish.' I bet I'd make a few dollars off that."

"Don't be disgusting," she said good-naturedly. "First and foremost, I would never sleep with a man I hardly know...at least I don't think I would. And second, the tabloids wouldn't buy that story unless we had sex and it miraculously brought back my memory *and* took place in a UFO filled with extraterrestrials."

The sound of his laughter was warm and deep and brought an involuntary smile to her slightly parted lips. She knew at that moment that nothing could dull *this* man's charm. Chase Lawson could make a snake smile.

"Who's that?" she asked, moving her head in the direction of an elderly gentleman standing off to one side speaking to an older woman.

"Jack David Gillian, Sr.," he responded. Sam's head tilted upward at the edge in his tone. "J.D. to his friends," he continued. "The man owns most of the county and has a rather ruthless reputation."

"Poor Mildred," Sam said in a quiet voice. "He sounds like he'll be an ogre as a father-in-law."

"Maybe back in the early days. According to Jack, Jr., Jack, Sr., is ill and little more than a shell of his former self. Which, believe me, wasn't pretty. He could be a hellish bastard if the mood struck," Chase said, then took another sip from his beer. "Even so, I guess it's good that J.D. doesn't realize his precious baby boy is going to marry a local girl."

"Hello, Samantha." A timid male voice interrupted their conversation.

Grudgingly, she turned away from the inviting sight of Chase grinning and looked in the direction of the speaker. "Michael Yester," she said after reading his name badge.

Extending his hand, Michael surprised her by asking her to dance.

"She promised this one to me," Chase interjected before she had an opportunity to respond to Michael's invitation.

Depositing his empty bottle along the way, Chase led her into the middle of the dance floor. He wrapped her in the circle of his arms, and her skin warmed where his fingers splayed across the bare skin.

"Why did you do that?" she asked, hoping conversation might help her to concentrate on something other than the way his thighs were brushing against hers as they swayed in time to the music.

Looking up at him, she spotted a devilish light burning in his eyes.

"Michael Yester is only after one thing."

"And you're not?"

He arched his eyebrows mockingly, and his sculpted lips curved slightly at each corner. "Not this time," he answered. His hand urged her forward, completely contradicting his remark.

"Really?" Sam countered in a sultry tone. "Then why are you holding me like this?"

His expression darkened and something indefinable briefly clouded his clear eyes. "We're dancing," he responded in a soft tone.

Sam thought about protesting but immediately saw the danger in doing so. If she admitted it felt like more than an innocent dance, it would mean her acknowledging to him that his nearness had a highly distracting effect. "If you say so," she whispered against his jacket.

"Actually, I *was* doing you a favor when I asked you to dance."

Gaping at him, Sam wondered if his unmitigated gall came as part of the package that had also provided the man with an incredible cleft in his chin. "What an arrogant thing to say."

"Honest," he countered with a crooked smile. "You see, Yester is still the same buffoon he was ten years ago." Sam tried not to smile at his assessment of the smaller man with the pocket protector and flood-ready polyester pants. "He didn't ask you to dance so that he could feel your incredibly soft skin. He just wanted to sell you a term life insurance policy. That's what ol' Mikey does these days, sells for Western Life and Health."

Sam couldn't help but laugh. The absurdity of buying insurance on a life you didn't remember was too ridiculous to be believed. "Thanks for acting in my best interests."

"I will, however, admit to a certain personal benefit I knew I would get from dancing with you." Chase's fingers fluttered up and down her spine, igniting tiny fires with each successive touch. Sam's body tensed as she tried to quell the desire rising in the pit of her stomach. "What's wrong?" he whispered into her hair. "Why are you as stiff as a board in my arms?"

"I guess I'm not used to dancing. In fact, I don't remember it at all."

"Relax and enjoy," Chase said. "Trust me."

Sam tried to relax, but she just couldn't manage it. Not with his hips moving against hers. Not with one of his hands playing with the sensitive skin at the nape of her neck, while the other teased the gentle slope of her waist.

She felt soft all over, and her feet dangled far above the ground as he guided her around the dance floor. On pure instinct, he slid his hands up the slope of her waist until he cradled her face, turning it upward. His eyes roamed over her delicate features, looking for any trace of trepidation before his mouth claimed hers.

Expertly, his tongue moistened her lower lip, and he felt her body shudder against him. Coaxing her lips apart, Chase explored the heated recesses of her mouth, all the while feeling his own body's quick and fervent response. His hands slid slowly lower as his mouth maintained control of hers. He felt the gentle taper of her throat where it melded with her collarbones. He was urged on by the groan of pleasure he heard as his hands moved even lower still. He felt the swell of her breasts as his fingers lingered at the edges of her rib cage. Again he was treated to the muffled sound of her moaning pleasure.

He wanted her then and there.

"Sam," he said against her mouth.

"We're in public," she said against his mouth.

"Which is the only reason I'm behaving like a gentleman," Chase said. Though he doubted the fantasies inspired by holding her against him and touching her could be remotely construed as gentlemanly.

There was definitely a change in her. That first time he'd kissed her, Sam had responded more with shock than interest. It was not like that anymore. There was passion and desire behind her motions now. Chase wanted to make love to her more than he wanted to take his next breath. It was a complication he hadn't expected—one he knew would only make his job more difficult.

Reluctantly, she left the comfort of his arms. Already their rather intimate dance had stirred up the curiosity of the crowd.

"Samantha!"

Connie was weaving her way across the dance floor, dragging an attractive man behind her.

"Hi," Sam said. "You look wonderful!"

"As do you," Connie said. "Tyler, Sam. Sam, Tyler."

The blond cowboy tipped his hat to her in greeting, then took Chase's outstretched hand.

"Good to see you again, Ty," Chase said.

"Same here. How's the horse business?"

"I need to go to the powder room," Sam whispered to Connie when the two men began to discuss animals.

"I'll be over there," Connie said, pointing to where Mildred and Jack stood chatting with J.D.

She discovered that she had to exit the front of the building and enter through a side door in order to find the facilities. Once inside the sanctuary of the ladies' room, Sam peered at her reflection and was surprised to find her face flushed from the encounter with Chase. Grabbing one of the paper towels from the silver dispenser on the wall, she fanned her face in an attempt to remove the stain of passion from her cheeks. *You're playing with fire, Sam,* she chastised herself silently.

"But what a wonderful fireplace," she whispered as she felt the giddy sensation grip her stomach. He was wonderful. There was just no way around it. And she wasn't going to let this opportunity pass her by. Not if she could help it.

Stepping out into the night air, Sam still wore the smile of a teenager in the first throes of love.

Love. The word and the concept filled her with the image of Chase. She hummed happily to herself as she made her way around the outside of the building.

She was almost at the end of the building when a man stepped into her path.

Startled, Sam's mind barely registered the cold finger of recognition. "You," she managed to say before he took his first ominous step from the shadows. This time, she didn't give in to her fear of being considered paranoid. She opened her mouth and screamed loud enough to wake the dead.

Apparently, he hadn't expected this reaction, since he immediately sprinted past her into the sanctuary of a wooded area behind the building. She was both relieved and terrified at the same time. Shaken, she leaned her trembling body against the wall for support.

That was where they found her.

"Sam! What happened?" Connie exclaimed.

Surrounded by Chase, Connie, Mildred and Jack, Sam no longer felt threatened. "I overreacted to the shadows," she insisted, though when her eyes found Chase's, she silently acknowledged there was more to it than that.

Chase instantly moved to place a comforting arm around her. "Next time," he whispered against her ear, "let me come with you."

Sam was somehow able to put the incident on the back burner for the remainder of the evening. She and Chase danced, talked, laughed, and by the time the event was nearing its end, Sam had conceded to herself that what she felt for Chase wasn't curiosity, gratitude or anything less than the first stirrings of deep emotion.

"Can you two pull yourselves apart long enough to help Mildred fill a few bags of trash?"

"No," Chase teased Connie.

"Please, Chase?" Connie pressed. "I think the lovebirds have had a tiff. Mildred's as sour as expired milk."

"We'll be there in a second," he promised the dark-haired woman. His arms tightened slightly. "I really don't want to help Mildred."

"I need to," Sam said with a sigh. "Because of the fire and the mysterious man in black, I wasn't any help with the preparations for the reunion."

"I want you to stay in here where I can see you," he instructed as they reluctantly stepped out of their embrace.

"You don't have to tell me twice," she assured him.

Connie's assessment of Mildred's mood was right on target. She seemed to be doing nothing but barking orders and expressing her displeasure with the entire volunteer staff. "I hope she doesn't nag Jack like this after the wedding," Connie whispered.

"Why is she so upset?" Sam inquired.

Connie shrugged as she shook open another plastic garbage bag. "Maybe J.D. had a lucid moment and told his son to call off the wedding."

"Why would he do that? Mildred's usually so sweet."

Connie chuckled. "Don't get me wrong, I love Mildred like a sister, but she has this controlling streak. In his earlier days, so did J.D. They would probably have killed each other inside a minute over some detail or other."

"She doesn't seem like a pushy woman," Sam defended.

"You didn't see her take on the zoning board over at Fairfield."

Sam's busy fingers stopped in midair. "Fairfield? Did you say Fairfield?"

"Yes."

"Fairfield Clinic?"

Connie's eyebrows arched questioningly. "Used to be, but that was years and years ago. I think we were still in school when the place went under. Some investment group bought it and wanted to open a medical research facility. Mildred made sure the old place stayed boarded up and deserted. She convinced everyone that the proposed use would flood our groundwater with toxic waste."

"How long has it been closed?"

Connie looked at the ceiling as she completed the calculation. "Eight or nine years. Her future father-in-law lost a fortune when she killed the zoning."

"WHAT DO YOU KNOW about the Fairfield Clinic?" Sam asked Chase the instant they were in the car and headed for his place.

"It was some sort of private hospital north of town."

"The Fairfield Clinic was one of the notations in my grandmother's diaries."

Chase scratched his chin. "Tell me more about the diaries."

She was careful to tell him every detail, ending with her suspicions about the key Karen had so innocently given her.

"I don't suppose you know if anyone besides you knew about the diaries?" he said.

"I didn't even know about them until that first morning. I mentioned them to you, and then I think I might have made some reference to them when we had lunch at Rafe's."

"But the key Karen gave you wasn't an exact match?"

"No."

"What about your outdoor visitor tonight?" Chase asked as he pushed open the door.

Sam immediately wrapped her arms around herself, feeling the chill from the encounter all over again. "The same deal. He wore a hood, so I can't tell you anything more than the fact that he's about your height and he apparently panics when I scream."

Chase didn't bother with the lights. Instead, he tossed aside his hat and jacket and pulled her to him. "I'm sorry I wasn't there for you," he said, as his lips moved against her hair.

"I'm glad it was over practically before it started. And thanks for not telling the others. I'm not sure I want my suspicions made public."

"I understand," he whispered as his hands strayed from her waist, moving slowly upward until he held her face in his large, gentle fingers. He studied her wide, expectant eyes before his full attention fell on her slightly parted lips. She saw just a flicker of indecision before his eyes closed and his mouth hungrily found hers.

For Sam, it was like a thousand explosions going off all at once. Her lips tingled where he traced their outline with the tip of his tongue. Her skin was on fire where he was pressed up against her. Her own hands began a slow, but determined, exploration of their own.

She could feel the muscles of his chest and stomach reacting to her feather-light touches. She could feel the rapid pulse racing through his system. She moved against him, the action coaxing a moan from his throat that gave her a heady feeling of power.

The pleasant scent of his cologne mingled with the other sensory messages vying for attention. His thumb stroked her cheek, gradually increasing the friction until even her face flamed with desire. He was so solid and yet his kiss was so tender, Sam couldn't decide which she liked better. It was all so very wonderful.

He tasted of alcohol as his mouth wove a magic spell on her lips. His hands left her face, traveling to the sensitive area just at the base of her throat. Sam arched her back in response to the fiery trail of kisses he left on her neck. His hands dipped lower still, until she felt the pressure of his hand through the filmy fabric of her dress.

She sucked in her breath when his palm flattened against the swell of her breast. His mouth moved back to hers, kissing her with the same urgency she felt propelling the slow gyrations of her hips against his.

"Please, Chase," she whispered, not at all sure what she was asking him for, but feeling as if she'd explode without it.

"I know," he said between kisses. "Believe me, I know," he said as his mouth left hers.

His hand slid away from her taut nipple, and his forehead rested against hers. For a moment, nothing passed between them except for their warm, labored breathing.

"I want—"

"Shh," he whispered, placing his finger against her oversensitized lips.

With the fog of passion clearing, Sam was more than a little surprised to see a look of regret in his dark eyes. "I don't understand," she said.

"We're going a little too fast, baby," he told her. "You've had more trauma in the past week or so than most people endure in a lifetime. Let's give it some time so we do it right."

She didn't want to do it right. She wanted to get close enough to him to become part of him. Unfortunately, she also knew he was being sensible.

When he kissed her again, it was different. It was sweet, gentle and very reassuring.

"An Investigator Dover from the arson squad called this morning," Chase told her as he handed her a cup of black coffee.

"And?"

He looked at her regretfully. "Inconclusive, but suspicious."

"Wonderful. Is there a way for them to investigate their suspicions?"

"They've done all the preliminary work and managed to find what they believe is the origin of the fire."

"Gasoline?" she suggested hopefully.

"Faulty wiring," he answered. "Apparently, one of the appliances shorted, causing a fire to start inside the studs."

"Do they know where it started?"

"The kitchen."

Sam felt a blanket of alarm begin to settle over her shoulders. "Let me guess," she said, meeting his eyes. "The coffeepot, right?"

"Right. It had a bad plug."

Sam fell back into the chair, but her eyes remained locked with his. "It most certainly did not. That first morning we were there, I had to plug it in myself. It was virtually brand-new and definitely *not* damaged in any way."

Chapter Nine

"You're losing my confidence."

"I'll admit there have been some problems with our initial plan, but I'm making adjustments now. I'm confident she'll no longer be a problem to you. She's going back to New York, and I can take care of her without there being a single connection to you."

"I've heard all this before. Stop talking about it and get the damn job done. I don't have a great deal of time left to spend on this problem. And remember, there's another loose end in New York."

"I'll take care of it. Relax."

"I'll be glad to relax when you've done what I'm paying you to do."

"Calm down. If you start to panic, this whole house of cards could collapse on top of you."

"You had better make sure that doesn't happen. I want this over. I don't have the luxury of time. If she remembers something before you take care of her, any additional work you do will be gratis. I've provided you with more than enough opportunities to take care of this. Now do it!''

"How LONG DID you know about the Gillian note?"

Chase sucked in an audible breath. He'd been expecting this question. "Burns told me about the note when he called me while you were still at Greenhaven."

She was staring out the car window, so he was spared those wide, inquisitive eyes that he knew held the power to bring the whole thing down on his head. The vivid memory of holding her—kissing her—made him tense with an odd mixture of pain and pleasure. *How can I do this to her?* The question seemed indelibly etched in his brain.

"I wonder if I was scribbling about the town, Senator Gillian or Jack, Sr.?"

"I'm afraid no one can answer that for you. I can tell you that Burns had no idea."

"Do you know why he didn't bother telling me?"

"I think it has something to do with tainting the evidence."

"Is there anything else you haven't told me?"

"I wasn't in New York when you were mugged, Sam," he said softly.

"I know," she said. "I'm sorry for bugging you about it."

"No problem," he managed to say. "Fairfield Clinic is just up ahead on the right."

Sam wasn't expecting the long, rectangular building surrounded by high weeds bordering what had once been a parking lot. A small square sign dangled off to one side, precariously hanging from a single rusted bolt. A red-and-white paper banner, tattered and slightly faded, indicated the building was available for purchase from Connie's real estate firm.

"Has it been vacant ever since the hospital closed?" she asked as they walked up the path, which was lined with overgrown shrubs and highway litter.

"That's what Connie told me when I picked up the key," he said as she opened the front door.

The interior was dark and smelled musty. Sam wasn't quite sure what she hoped to find, she was just praying it would jump out at her as they went along.

Wind from a partially broken pane caused scraps of paper to flutter in the hallway. She kept her body close to his, fearful of the eerie silence in the forsaken building.

"This was obviously a waiting area," she surmised.

"Very good."

"I know my way around hospitals," she assured him. Sam looped both her arms through one of his.

They were faced with a choice as they moved farther inside. Shrugging, Sam indicated with a head movement for them to go left. Her only guide was a small painted arrow, indicating that the office had once been in the area they were about to explore.

"There's nothing here but trash," she noted as they peeked into a few of the rooms. There were a few lengths of tubing, the occasional bunch of wires, but very little else to indicate what had gone on in the hospital that might have inspired her grandmother to mention it in her diary.

They retraced their steps and tried the other hallway. It was pretty much the same, except for the last two sections. One section had quite obviously been a cluster of operating rooms. One room even had the dusty light fixture still dangling over the place where the operating table must have been.

The second section was a bit more perplexing. It was longer than the other rooms, and one wall was partitioned off so that the top half might have been glass. "Maybe this was some sort of lounge or social area," Sam suggested.

"You got me," Chase said just before he bent down to retrieve a pale blue piece of molded plastic.

"It looks as if Connie needs to arrange to have this place cleaned," Sam noted.

Chase nodded. "Seen enough?"

"I guess," she told him reluctantly. "Sorry for dragging you all the way out here."

"No problem, but we'd better get back if we're going to get to the airport in time for the flight."

SAM AND CHASE FLEW into New York, rented a car and drove northeast in the direction of Middletown, a small town near Greenwood Lake. The lake itself was shared by the states of New York and New Jersey. Karen's family lived just inside the New York line. The industrial landscape soon gave way to small mountains and rugged cliffs where the roadway curved like a hurried snake.

They arrived just as the late-summer sun dipped behind one of the mountains to the west. Chase stopped in front of a nondescript motel on Route 17.

"Stay here, I'll go in and register us."

"As Mr. and Mrs. Smith?" Sam teased with a wink as she pushed open the car door and joined him. "Just kidding, Chase. Separate rooms."

"You're no fun," he grumbled as they walked into the office of the Red Rose Motel.

A woman Sam guessed to be somewhere close to the age of the planet hoisted her rotund body from a chair. The scent of chocolate filled the room, and Sam's eyes were drawn to the half-eaten box of frosted doughnuts on the table next to a small black-and-white television.

"Help yous?"

A vision of a room flashed across her brain, then disappeared. "Do you have any rooms with rust-colored carpets and olive-green paint on the walls?" Her words came out in a flurry of syllables.

The old woman's forehead stiffened into rows of deep crevices separated by small rolls of fat. "All of our rooms are like that."

"Have you seen me before?" Sam asked, reaching out and grabbing hold of one pudgy wrist.

"Sure," the woman answered matter-of-factly.

Sam felt her heartbeat increase with excitement. Apparently, this was a real memory!

"You're that girl from *Secret Splendor* who got mugged."

Sam's heart fell to her feet. "That's not what I meant," she said, refusing to loosen her grip on the woman's wrist. "Have you seen me here? At this motel?"

"Nope. But I only just come back to work. Spend my winters in Florida. Got a nice trailer over on the West Coast near—"

"We'd like two rooms," Chase interrupted. "Adjoining, if possible."

Reluctantly, Sam let go of the woman's wrist so that she could complete the paperwork necessary for them to rent rooms.

"Want to tell me what that was all about?" Chase asked as they pulled their small suitcases from the car.

"Wait until you unlock the door to the room. You'll find two double beds against one wall, rust-colored carpeting, a vinyl easy chair, a television, a nightstand and a dresser. On top of the dresser you'll find a card and envelope to tip the maid. And the curtains don't fit the windows, so there is always a crack of light streaming through during daylight."

When Chase opened the door to Sam's room, he let out a low whistle. It was just as she described. "Apparently, you *have* been here before."

"Apparently," she parroted. Moving past him, she tossed her bag on one of the beds and tried to ignore the musty odor.

"Do you think you might have come up here with Karen?"

"That may be the answer. But I'll warn you now, in the morning I'll probably forget that I ever remembered this place."

After they were settled, they wandered across the four-lane highway and entered a small restaurant. The place was a deserted rectangle with a counter that spanned the length of the room. Behind the counter was a grill and all the necessary equipment for food preparation. A middle-aged man was behind the counter, his face partially obscured by a newspaper.

Sam and Chase decided to sit at the counter. No sense in making the man walk the distance to one of the tables since they were the only customers.

"What can I get yous folks?" he asked, folding his newspaper neatly and stuffing it beside an antiquated cash register. "Why I never thought I'd see you again!" he exclaimed as he looked at Sam for the first time, his face blanching.

"Really?" Sam asked, befuddled.

"Considering what happened the last time, I didn't think you'd be able to stomach coming back here."

"What happened the last time she was here?" Chase asked.

The man looked to Sam, who gave him a nod to go ahead and tell whatever it was that had turned his skin that ashen color.

"Her and a girlfriend was in here having breakfast, I'd say on about a year ago now—give or take. Her girlfriend handed her a package and then got up to go back over to the motel. That's when the car hit her. She must have flown fifty feet in the air. Dead before her body even hit the pavement."

The two of them ate in virtual silence. Chase watched helplessly as she spent most of the meal pushing a bit of sausage around a chipped china plate with a fork that had all its tines askew. The counterman's graphic story was enough for even Sam to know that he had described Grace's violent demise.

"What were Grace and I doing here in New York the week before I was mugged?"

"I don't think anyone ever found that out. All I know is that the police ruled it a hit and run."

Sam's head whipped up, and she turned her eyes on Chase. Just as he had suspected, they were narrowed with strong and sudden accusation. "You knew Grace died here?"

Reaching down on the seat next to him, Chase picked up his Stetson and made a production out of straightening the brim. He prayed for a convincing and easy lie.

"I asked you a question," she prodded.

"Yes," he finally responded in a soft tone. He was tired of lying.

"How could you do such a thing? I mean, you knew this is where Grace died, and you didn't think you should warn me?"

"I wasn't sure how you'd react."

She seemed to accept his lame excuse.

Taking in a breath, Sam lowered her head and wordlessly followed him from the restaurant. "This is good," she decided. "This might be the place where everything started."

"Sam, sweetheart," Chase said as he turned and grasped her shoulders. "There was a complete investigation into the accident. The police didn't find a thing."

"Maybe they weren't looking in the right direction."

"Karen's funeral is going to be tough on you. Do you really think it's a good idea to rehash what I'm sure was a terrible ordeal for you?"

She showed her appreciation for his concern by gently stroking the side of his face. "I haven't got much else to go on, Chase. The diaries are soaked through from the fire. Fairfield Clinic was a bust. Every time one of these little accidents happen, I lose another piece of myself. I need to make some sense out of all this."

She watched as his eyes displayed his inner conflict. While it was sweet and very encouraging to think that he wanted to shield her from the past, she needed to go forward. She was still thinking about how she would do this as they approached the motel. "I'd like to check something out at the motel office," he said as they walked by the motel sign.

"What something?" Sam prodded.

"Go back to your room and lock the door. I'll be back as quickly as I can." She had taken a single step toward the room when Chase reached out and grabbed her arm. The kiss was quick, but enjoyable nonetheless.

"Don't open the door for anyone but me," he said, tapping his finger against her upturned nose.

"I'll behave," she promised him just before jogging over to her room.

Pulling a fifty-dollar bill from his pocket, Chase walked into the office and asked the clerk for receipts of any long-distance calls Grace had received while she was staying at the motel the previous year. The woman seemed excited at the prospect of filling the request.

SAM WATCHED from the window long after he had disappeared inside the dreary little office. "Beautiful," she muttered, then felt guilty for having a carnal thought when it was apparent that Chase wanted them to slow things down.

Sam had been watching Chase so intently that she barely noticed the tan sedan pull into the spot on the other side of their rental vehicle. The man behind the wheel was dressed in black, hooded and, obviously, heading for her door.

Sam rushed into the bathroom and locked the door behind her. She could hear the sounds of the man tampering with the room lock. "Why didn't I call the desk?" Sam asked herself as she paced in front of the yellowed porcelain tub. She raised her eyes, praying for divine intervention, when the answer to her unspoken prayer appeared. *The window.*

Sam had to climb onto the edge of the pedestal sink in order to reach the opening. She stopped every few seconds to listen for sounds of the stranger's progress, but it was hard to hear him over the pulse pounding in her ears. *Please come back, Chase!* she silently implored as she struggled with the corroded lock on the window.

Her hand slipped, and Sam felt a splinter force its way under her fingernail. The pain was terrible but the least of her worries at the moment. Sucking on her injured finger, Sam was teetering on the rounded edge of the sink when she heard the outer door opening. He was going to succeed this time, she realized, as she made one final, futile attempt to turn the lock. Tears of frustration welled up in her eyes, making it almost impossible for her to keep sight of her objective.

Scream! her brain commanded.

The sound echoed in the small room, very nearly drowning out the splintering of wood when the frame collapsed from the other side.

"It's me, Sam."

"Chase!" She jumped into his arms, burying her face against him as the tears rolled down her face. "He was here," she said, sobbing.

"Your man in black?" he asked as he carried her to the edge of the bed. "Did you get a look at him this time?"

"No," she said between sniffles. "Do you think we ought to call Detective Burns?"

After checking outside the window, Chase stroked her back until her trembling subsided. "You can if you want to."

"You don't think it's a good idea?"

He stroked her hair. "No one's actually seen this guy but you."

"You're right," she said against his shirt.

Chase could feel the warm moisture of her tears and felt his own body knot with frustration. How long could he keep this up? These incidents were beginning to take their toll on both of them. It was killing him to see the anxiety in her eyes and know in his heart that he was to blame.

"Feel better?"

"Yeah," she answered, dabbing her eyes with the back of her hand. "I saw a man get out of a car and come toward this room. I ran into the bathroom and that's when I heard someone at the door. Did you see anyone when you were returning from the office?"

"Sorry."

Sam slipped away from him and moved to the window. The car was gone. She opened the door and examined the lock. Nothing. "Maybe I'm imagining all this," she said, her shoulders slumped. She didn't dare turn to look at him. "You're right, I'm the only one who has ever seen this man in black."

"I'm sure he's real."

His words of encouragement couldn't totally erase the doubts lingering in her mind. He came up behind her then, wrapping his arms around her in a comforting cocoon of warmth. She felt his breath spill over her neck. Sam was treated to several agonizingly precious minutes of his body against hers. Reaching up, her hands caressed his forearms where they crossed in front of her. She was beginning to recognize the subtle change in his breathing. She could also tell by the rigid way he was holding her that he had no intention of going back on his decision to slow down the pace.

Sam wanted nothing more than to turn and feel his lips against hers, to lose herself in the flames of sensations he so easily ignited in her body. "I don't want comfort from you," she said.

"What do you want?"

"I'm not sure," she admitted as her fingernail traced the edge of the silver button at his cuff. "I know I feel wonderful when you kiss me and touch me. I think you do, too."

She felt the kiss he placed on top of her head. "I never said I didn't want those things, Sam. I just want things between us to be right first."

There was a sadness in his voice.

"How do they get right?"

"They'll be right when all this stuff is behind us. If you feel the same way once you've gotten all your answers, you won't hear any argument from me."

"What about you? You make it sound as if I'm the one applying the brakes here."

"Please know that I want you, Sam. If you don't believe anything else, believe that."

She squeezed his hand. "If we both want the same thing, why are we pretending that we don't?"

"I'd be a real heel if I took you up on your offer now."

"I still don't understand," she said, a pleading note in her tone.

"You will," he assured her hollowly.

"Will you hold me for awhile if I promise not to make any inappropriate moves?"

His low laughter filled some of the empty ache. "Always," he told her.

When he turned her, Sam spotted the papers sticking out of his shirt pocket. "What's this?"

"Come and let me show you."

Her curiosity had maneuvered her right out of his arms. *Not a very swift move for someone positively smitten,* she chided.

Chase pulled the rumpled paper from his pocket. There was just the slightest tremor in his hand, and he hoped she wouldn't notice.

"This is your number in New York," he confirmed. "This is Mildred's number," he added, pointing to another number on the page. "And this one has an Arizona area code, but I don't recognize the number, do you?"

"No," Sam said in a husky voice that rekindled the ache in his groin.

"Let's call it and see what we get." Chase was careful to dial exactly. On the seventh ring, the phone was answered by a juvenile-sounding voice.

"Hi, is your mother or father home?"

"No, they're in buying groceries."

"And they left you home alone?"

"Heck no, mister. My folks ain't dumb."

"If you're not at home, where are you?"

"At the pay phone outside the U-Bag Market on Main Street."

"Main Street where?"

"Gillian, Arizona."

Chapter Ten

As they drove down the highway, Sam was beginning to feel as if she wasn't doing much more than creating additional questions in her mind. "Why would I have met Grace in Middletown? And why did she call a pay phone in Gillian?"

Chase didn't respond to her questions; apparently, he realized she was thinking aloud, trying to get some sense of understanding. "If everything is connected to Gillian, why was I attacked in Central Park? Or Patty in San Diego?" Her arms circled in wild gestures, simulating the circular thoughts going around in her brain.

"Are we back to the conspiracy theory?" Chase asked.

Sam's hands grew still. "I know it sounds far-fetched," she admitted, "but I know there's something that ties all of this together."

"Such as?"

"Such as . . . Gillian," she said. "We were all from Gillian."

"What about Karen?"

The twinge of pain in her heart was eclipsed by the determination of her newfound convictions. "Guilt by association."

"Come again?"

"Have you always been so negative?" she said, exasperated.

He only shrugged.

"There has to be something Karen knew about me. Or maybe someone thought she knew something and that made them murder her."

"If that's true, why wasn't she killed right around the time you were mugged?"

Sam felt her body deflate. "If I knew that, I'd know why she was killed *and* by whom."

"Even if I concede you that point, there's still the matter of Patty. Not to mention the logistics of pulling all this off."

"When was Patty killed in relation to Grace's death and my attack?"

She watched the flicker of emotion pass in his dark eyes before he answered. "Two weeks before Grace. About three weeks before you were mugged."

"So everything happened all at once."

"Just about."

She could feel the tension from his body and regretted questioning him. This was obviously very upsetting for Chase. His long fingers gripped the wheel so hard that his bronzed knuckles had turned pale. His posture was stiff and as rigid as his chiseled expression.

Feeling frustrated, and realizing the effect her conversation was having on him, Sam decided to let it go—for now.

Chase took her directly to the police station, which was a small, nondescript building down a winding mountain road.

Touching his shirtsleeve, Sam said, "You don't have to go in with me if this is too painful for you."

"I'm tough," he said, though there was a definite distance in his eyes that even his hat couldn't hide.

The sound of their footsteps echoed through the corridor of the building. Stopping at the first desk she came to, Sam introduced herself and asked to speak to the officer in charge of the investigation into Grace Morningdew's death.

"That would be Detective Manetti," the desk officer said. "But that case was closed."

"We know that," Chase said as he placed his hand at the small of Sam's back.

"Third door on the left," the officer said with a tired voice.

After thanking him, they went in search of Detective Manetti. She was surprised to find a fairly young-looking man in a crisp white shirt and bold paisley tie sitting with his feet up on the desk. He was busy crumpling paper wads and tossing them into a makeshift hoop above a trash can. Lying about the basket on all sides were many of the paper wads that had apparently missed their mark.

When he failed to notice them, Sam loudly cleared her throat.

He snapped to an upright position, his face turning a deep red before he rose and extended his hand. "Nice to see you again, Ms. Parrish."

Sam's breath stopped as if she'd been struck. "We've met?" she asked the young man with dark hair, dark eyes and a light olive complexion.

"I handled...oh right, I forgot about your mugging in the city."

"So have I," Sam responded in an attempt to make the man feel more at ease. "Detective Manetti, would you mind going over with me what happened outside the restaurant on the day my...Grace Morningdew was killed?"

She watched as his dark features wrinkled. "That's more than a year ago now."

She watched Chase's eyes glance in the direction of the basketball setup, then to the detective. "Can we have a look at the reports."

"Certainly, Mr.—"

"Lawson," he said, abruptly extending his hand across the desk to shake Manetti's.

The detective's expression looked odd to Sam. Perhaps he was intimidated by Chase. The handshake seemed to take a fraction too long, but then Sam decided she was probably just being impatient.

"Let me run and get the file. Please have a seat, it won't take but a minute."

The chairs were cold gray metal with built-in seat cushions that had long ceased functioning as pads against the hard frame. There were no arms on the chair, so Sam folded her hands over her purse and stared out the window. She could easily make out the outline of the mountains on either side of the building. She could also see Chase in her peripheral vision. The stiff set of his jaw made her feel remorseful for having dragged him with her to reopen this old wound. A small part of her heart ached at the thinly veiled sadness in his eyes.

"Got the file."

The sound of the detective's voice jarred her from her musings and threw her back into the grim reality of the task at hand.

"The file was with my lieutenant," Manetti said to Chase. "He may come by to see you. He seemed pretty surprised that you'd shown up here."

"Why is that?" Sam asked.

"I guess it's because so much time has passed," Chase answered hurriedly.

Sam reached for the file but the detective stopped her from taking it off his desk.

"Ms. Parrish, I think you ought to let me take the pictures out before you go riffling through this... there's some pretty gruesome stuff here."

Nodding, Sam waited until he had extracted all the photos and placed them facedown on his desk. He then handed her a rather tattered and flimsy manila folder. She was shocked to find only three statements in the file—hers, the detective's and the counterman's. There was an autopsy report, which made her think of the odd similarity to Karen's fate.

It took her no time at all to realize that the man from the restaurant had basically told her everything there was to tell. A car had apparently been speeding down the incline, made the curve, but then, they speculated, he'd veered off onto the shoulder, hitting Grace just before she stepped into the street. It sounded so much like the incident she and Chase had experienced in Manhattan that Sam shuddered and flipped to the next page.

"I'll be right back," Chase said as he rose and left the room.

Sam was involved in reading through the statements, so she merely mumbled something unintelligible.

"There was never any follow-up?" she asked Manetti.

"What should we have followed up on?" he answered. He frowned, as if her inquiry into the long-closed matter was bothersome. "You'll note that there was no forensic evidence and that none of the witnesses—*including you*—could ID the car."

Sam swallowed and looked at the detective. "I'm sorry. I wasn't questioning the way the matter was handled. I just wondered if your office was aware of the fact that just a couple of weeks before this accident, another woman from Gillian died in California?"

"I—"

"Ms. Parrish, I'm Lieutenant Ginsberg."

Turning in her seat, Sam politely smiled up at the man who had burst in. Chase entered just behind him and returned to his seat. The lieutenant, a fit-looking man who she guessed was somewhere in his early fifties stepped between them and leaned against the desk.

"Lieutenant," she said as she offered her hand. "This is Chase Lawson."

The man inclined his head slightly and said, "We met in the hall."

"I was just telling Detective Manetti about another young woman that died in an accident two weeks before Grace did."

He stroked the slight stubble on his chin. "A Patricia Sanders?"

"Sands," she corrected.

"Yes," Ginsberg stated with a nod of recognition.

"You knew?" Sam asked.

Manetti was no longer visible to her, but Sam sensed a definite strain coming from somewhere.

"You told us," Ginsberg replied.

"Is it part of my statement?"

"I believe it's toward the end."

Riffling through the crisp pages, Sam found a single sentence that indicated she had, indeed, mentioned Patty's death to the police. Reading further, Sam was startled that she had stated her reason for being in Middletown was to pick up a diary from Grace.

"Why would we have met in Middletown when I had an apartment in New York?" Sam asked.

"You didn't know a year ago, either," Ginsberg answered.

"Do you still have the diary?" she asked.

"No. We looked at it and gave you back the key and the diary."

Immediately, Sam's hand went to the key dangling on the chain beneath her blouse. "Was this the key?" she asked hopefully, tossing the file on his desk and pulling up the key for his inspection.

"Looks like it, but I couldn't swear to it."

"Did you happen to take pictures of the diary or the key?"

"They were yours, Ms. Parrish. They didn't belong to the deceased."

"But she had just given them to me!" Sam implored.

"And she had just eaten breakfast, but we didn't go into the diner and photograph all the toast," he said testily.

Ginsberg's neck had turned red, and Sam supposed her questions had been interpreted as a personal criticism. "I didn't mean to belittle the performance of your department, Lieutenant. I'm just frustrated because I can't remember, so I need other people to fill in the details for me."

"I'm afraid those are all the details we have."
Ginsberg pushed away from the desk and extended his
hand in her direction. "I'm sorry we couldn't have
been more help to you."

"Thank you," she said without really feeling much
gratitude. This was yet another in a long line of dead
ends. When she felt Chase's hand at her elbow, Sam
mumbled a farewell and allowed Chase to lead her in
the direction of the door. Sam stopped and turned
slowly.

"Do you know the Quinn family?" she asked.

"No," Ginsberg said. Manetti just shook his head.

"Their daughter, Karen, was a friend of mine. She
had an accident, too. Her funeral is tomorrow."

IT WASN'T just a funeral, it was a zoo. In spite of the
fact that she had draped a scarf over her head and
worn large, dark glasses, the cameras began clicking
the minute she emerged from the car. Total strangers
followed them as they climbed the stone staircase in
front of the church. Solemn music and the scent of
incense was almost as overpowering as finding herself
the center of attention. She silently thanked the image on the cross for the man at her side.

When several heads turned in her direction, Chase
gave her shoulders a reassuring squeeze. They sat near
the middle of the ornate church. Sam hoped the interest of the other mourners would pass before the
beginning of the service. Luckily, there was no coffin
to stare at. She tried to calm her frazzled nerves by

counting the hundreds of blossoms displayed on the altar. It worked.

Sam was secretly relieved to discover this was to be a memorial service. It saved her from having to deal with the finality of death. Three brothers and two sisters spoke of a loving childhood with Karen. It was a bittersweet event that had her alternating between tears and smiles.

The Quinns seemed to be handling it as best they could. Sam recognized them from the pictures Karen always carried in her wallet—group photos were a Quinn tradition. Karen had complained about having them taken, and then, of course, she'd never liked herself in any of the end results.

"Which child was the accident?" she would ask. "The one that's seventeen years younger than her closest sibling, perhaps?"

Sam smiled at the memory. Karen wasn't upset by the large gap—not really. You could tell that she loved her family, and Sam recalled that she spoke often of wanting to be rich and famous so that she could care for her elderly parents. She felt she owed them something for having sacrificed their forties and fifties raising their unexpected daughter. Sam glanced at the people in the front row, trying to guess which of the brothers was the one who had dubbed Karen "Major Mistake."

Mistake. Sam stiffened at the thought. Karen had said something about making a mistake. What could she have meant?

"We're gathering downstairs. Will the two of you be joining us for coffee?"

The invitation had come from Katherine, Karen's beautiful and dignified mother. Sam marveled at the woman's composure and politely accepted her gracious invitation.

The lower floor of the church was a large room lined with childlike works of art and posters announcing various church activities. At the far end of the room was an open doorway that led to modest kitchen facilities. Pushing the scarf from her head, Sam glanced around the room looking for Charlie.

"I wonder where he is," she murmured.

"Who?" Chase asked.

"Charlie Newsome ... You'd think he would have had the decency to pay his respects to the family," she whispered.

"Maybe he was running low on hair spray," Chase whispered against her ear.

"I'm going to see if I can lend a hand in the kitchen," she told him. "Do you mind?"

"Go ahead," Chase told her with a smile that reached all the way to his eyes.

When he looked at her like that, Sam felt safe and secure. Trying to recall the past didn't seem so important. The possibility of a future with Chase was a far superior alternative.

"It was so nice of you to come," a woman who identified herself as Karen's sister Kelly said.

"I just wish there was something I could do."

Kelly's green eyes looked tired, and the gray appeared to be overtaking the red in her hair. "It hurts but we'll get through it, Miss Parrish."

Sam had no doubt but that they would. "Please call me Sam."

"Okay, Sam," Kelly agreed easily. "Are you any good at pouring coffee?"

Grateful for a task, Sam nodded and deposited her handbag on the shiny metal counter. "Please go spend time with your family," she insisted. "I'll take care of this."

Sam could see Chase from her vantage point in the kitchen. He was talking to a man with a dark hat. At first, Sam mistook the deep lines at Chase's forehead for concern. On closer scrutiny, Sam recognized the dark cloud of anger in his eyes. *What on earth...?* she wondered. "Ouch!" she cried. In watching Chase, she had neglected to keep tabs on her duties. Consequently, the moderately hot coffee had overflowed the paper cup and spilled over onto her hand. Moving to the sink, Sam ran cool water on the injury and soon decided that it wasn't anything major. When she turned back, Chase and the man were gone.

She didn't think much of it at first. Between filling cups, Sam scanned the assembled group fully expecting to catch sight of him in the sea of black. He should not have been hard to find—Chase was quite a contrast to the fair-skinned redheads who dominated Karen's family on both sides.

When she was no longer needed in the kitchen, Sam set off in search of her escort. Several minutes later, when she had looked everywhere except the men's room, Sam began to experience tiny twinges of worry. "Where could he have gone?"

"Who?"

The source of the question was the priest, and Sam immediately responded. "My escort. He's a tall man, wearing a Western-cut suit, snakeskin boots, Native American—"

"I believe he and another gentleman went out into the interment area."

"As in cemetery?" she asked.

"Yes." He smiled at her slightly rattled tone. "It's through that door."

At least there were no paparazzi in the cemetery. None that she could see, anyway. With her scarf billowing in the warm breeze, Sam scanned the peaceful setting. There were a lot of ivory-covered markers, but no Chase. About twenty yards down a stone path, Sam spotted a building. It was covered by some sort of vine with delicate blue flowers, which she purposefully stared at as she made her way through the still cemetery.

Large trees stood guard over the dead, their branches danced with the shadows and caused a faint rustling sound. Sam walked faster. She glanced back when she heard a loud cracking sound. When she failed to see anything, she swallowed her anxiety and concentrated on her destination.

Her hand gripped the ornamental iron handle on the weathered wooden door. It took a great deal of effort before she was able to coax it fully open.

"That's probably her."

"Chase?" she called softly into the darkened mausoleum.

"Back here," he said.

Sam followed the sound of his voice and quickly reached him. "What are you doing out here?" she asked.

"Looking around."

"Who were you talking to?"

"Me?" His hand draped lazily over her shoulder, and he turned her back toward the entrance. "No one."

"I heard a man's voice."

"It was me."

"Who were you talking to? Aren't these all crypts?"

"I was just reading one of the inscriptions."

"How could you be reading? It's too dark in here to see the floor."

"I—"

The small triangle of light at the door began to shrink.

"Hey!" Chase called before sprinting ahead.

He was too late. The door had closed, plunging them into total darkness.

"Chase?"

"I'm here!" he yelled back. "Dammit!"

"What?" she asked when she finally felt him in front of her.

"The door is stuck."

"We're trapped in here with all these dead people?"

Chase's arm came out and gently urged her against the cold wall. "I don't want to ram you."

"What are you going to do?" she asked as her eyes finally picked out his outline.

"Give it a good shove. It's probably just stuck."

There was a terrible thud, followed by a string of expletives.

"We're trapped, aren't we?" she asked fearfully.

"I'm working on it," he mumbled.

Another thud, another grunt, and several more expletives. Sam thought she heard movement toward the back of the room.

"Keep working," she told him.

After several more fruitless attempts, she could hear his labored breaths.

"Now what?"

"Now we yell," Chase instructed her.

The two of them made a racket that echoed off the walls. Sam had to place her hands over her ears in order to continue.

"This isn't working," she told him in a raspy voice.

"Hush!" he commanded softly.

Immediately, she heard sounds from the other side. "In here!" she yelled, placing her palms and ear against the door.

"Just a second!"

The door opened slowly. Too slowly for Sam, who stood in the small filter of light until there was just enough room for her to slide out.

"I wonder how that could have happened," the priest was saying. He had a large branch in his hand, which had obviously been lodged against the door handle and the ground. Looking up, they could see that it hadn't fallen from any of the trees above. It wasn't the same variety.

"The wind?" Chase suggested.

"Who knows?" the priest answered. "I hope you two didn't get a scare."

"No problem," Chase replied.

"You could have gone out the back," the priest suggested.

Sam's mouth gaped open.

"Like him."

Sam looked in the direction the priest was pointing and caught only a fleeting view of a man in a dark suit. "He was in there with us?"

"He came out the back as you came out the front," the priest said.

When she looked at Chase, he only shrugged. "I didn't know there was a back door."

"DO YOU THINK someone put that limb there to trap us inside?" she asked when they were in the car.

"That wouldn't have been too smart," he said. "If we'd have known, we could have just waltzed out the back."

"Why didn't the other guy waltz out the back while we were in there screaming our fool heads off?"

"Calm down, Sam," he said, patting her knee with one hand. "Maybe it was just some kids fooling around. You've got to stop looking for trouble where none exists."

"What about the man?"

"I think the good father was mistaken. I didn't see anyone when I was in there."

Sam wanted to argue, but she knew she'd only wind up sounding like an irrational fool. Besides, he was probably right, anyway.

"Still want to drive to your apartment?" he asked.

"Definitely. I don't want to spend another second in that motel." She shivered in her seat.

"NICE TO SEE YOU, Miss Parrish."

"Thank you," she greeted the doorman.

"This came for you while you were in Arizona. We got your telegram about the fire, so I've been holding this at the desk."

Sam turned the small package over in her hand as they ascended in the elevator. There was a New York postmark but no return address. The word "PERSONAL" was written in a familiar hand.

Following Chase, she entered her apartment and went directly into the kitchen, grabbed a knife and opened the package.

"Chase! Look at this!"

"What is it?"

"It's from Karen."

Chapter Eleven

"It's a tape," she said, turning the microcassette over in her hand.

"Do you have a tape player?"

"In the bedroom."

"Come on," he said and took her hand to lead her to the bedroom.

Sam got the machine out of a drawer and handed it to Chase. He lifted the compartment, extracted a near-identical tape from her machine, replaced it with the one Karen had sent and pressed play.

"If you don't bring the diary tonight, they'll kill her."

"That's Charlie's voice!"

"Shh."

"Meet me in Central Park tonight at two o'clock. The jogging path."

Chase played the tape a second time while Sam stood by hugging her chest. "Who will they kill?" she asked. "And who are they?"

Chase was shaking his head. "And why would they go through Newsome?"

"I got a lot of cards and messages through Charlie when I was in the hospital. I guess people used to contact him to get to me."

Chase rose and shrugged out of his jacket. She looked as if she'd been punched in the gut, and he didn't have the first clue what to do about it.

"Did he ever mention this to you?"

Sam shook her head. "He only came to visit a couple of times. Maybe he said something to Detective Burns who never told me."

"Not likely. This tape would have given Burns a solid lead."

"How did Karen get it?"

"Beats me. But I think this was what she was talking about when she said she had made a mistake."

She looked up at him, her eyes were raw and brimming with tears. He felt as if a knife had just sliced through his chest.

"Do you think she's known about this all along?" Sam asked in a soft voice. "What if she only spent time with me to make sure she was around in case I remembered?"

"Sam," he said as he gathered her against him, "this tape is damning for Newsome. But there's nothing on there to indicate Karen had anything to do with it."

"Then how did she get it?"

"I think we should ask your friend Charlie that."

He felt her nod, but he was reluctant to let her go. He had to, though, he had to make a call. "Why don't you go in and splash some water on your face?"

"Okay."

"I'll make you some tea, and then we can figure out what to do from here."

When she was safely behind the closed bathroom door, Chase dialed, cupping his hand over his mouth to muffle any sound. On the third ring, he heard the water stop.

"Great," he grumbled, hanging up the phone. He pocketed the tape and made a dash for the kitchen.

When she joined him, the color was still missing from her cheeks, but she no longer looked on the verge of tears. He rolled up his sleeves and foraged for ingredients. Sam dejectedly sat at the table, her hands clasped together.

"I think we should go see Charlie," she suggested.

"You're not going anywhere."

She stared at his back, her eyebrows drawn tightly together. "But he obviously knows something, Chase. I want to know what it is."

"So we'll give it to Burns."

"Not this time," she told him emphatically. "I'm tired of letting other people take control of my life. What if Charlie is being threatened, as well? What if he couldn't go to the police because he knows that whoever is doing this might hurt him?"

He shook his head. "The cops could protect him." He turned, meeting her eyes. "I know you don't want to believe that your friend is involved with this, Sam. But I think the tape pretty much verifies that he is."

His expression was kind and gentle, and Sam silently acknowledged that she would have been lost without him. *God, I love you!* she thought—though she didn't dare say so aloud.

"Humor me, Chase. Can't we just talk to him before we call the police?"

There was a flicker of indecision in his eyes, and she held her breath—hoping.

"Just talk, huh?"

"I promise. I just want him to tell me how he could do this."

"And if Karen knew?" he finished.

Sam stood and closed the small space between them. "I need to know that. I don't want to believe that all this time I've been a fool, but I have to know."

"Thinking the best of a friend doesn't make you a fool. Besides, people sometimes do the wrong thing for the right reason."

Reaching up, Sam gently ran the tip of her finger-nail near the bottom of his lower lip. She could feel the outline of his powerfully built thighs where they rubbed hers. "There's never a right time to lie," she told him.

"There are many shades of gray in this world."

His expression stilled and grew serious when Sam pressed herself against him. Chase dropped the tea bag he'd been holding and placed his hands at her waist. For an instant, she thought he might push her away.

"Not this time," she beseeched. "Please?"

His hesitation lasted less than a second before his lips found hers. Tentative and testing, his mouth settled over hers. She responded by allowing her lips to part, urging his sweet exploration. He groaned as his arms encircled her, pulling her so close that Sam could feel every solid inch of him.

Her mind reeled from the blatant sensuality of his kiss. It was as if a flash fire had ignited, and it was quickly burning out of control. Her hands moved down from his face until she could feel the circle of his medallion over the spot where his heart beat furiously. He gripped her more tightly, causing her back to arch. Chase moaned against her mouth.

Emotions and sensations melted together and coursed through her veins. Every cell in her body tingled with life, and she began to work on the buttons of his shirt. Guided by the powerful force of her desire,

Sam pushed aside the fabric and ran her palms over his warm flesh. His breath fell hotly over her skin when he lifted his head. She was about to utter a protest when he lifted her off the ground and carried her toward the bedroom.

His lips were on her throat, tasting the faintly floral scent of her skin. She felt so delicate, and yet the strength of her passion had completely obliterated his resolve. He didn't want to think about it now. If he did, he knew he'd have to stop. *Not this time.*

He placed her on the bed and lay beside her, his one leg wedged between hers. Placing his hand at her waist, Chase kissed the tip of her nose before renewing his interest in her throat. He felt her intake of breath when his fingers inched upward then closed over her rounded breast. He could feel the taut nipple pressing against his palm and that knowledge sent waves of urgent desire to his loins. Each caress seemed to make her want more, and he was more than willing to give it.

Slowly, deliberately, he toyed with each button, kissing the areas as they were exposed to his hungry eyes. Her skin was smooth, rich and pale under his hand. Chase was finding it hard to exercise discipline. Lifting his head, he looked at her flushed face briefly before turning his attention lower. Her feathery fingers fanned out across his chest as he loomed above her, eyes fixed on her lacy black bra. His finger dipped inside the garment, teasing the hard nipple. It wasn't enough.

Undoing the clasp, Chase peeled away the barrier. She made a small sound when his mouth closed around the tip of her breast. Her hands tangled in his hair, holding him against her as she arched upward, toward him.

Each time he flicked the tip of her nipple with his tongue, Sam moaned and pressed her hips against his leg.

Pulling at her skirt, Chase reached beneath it and placed his hand on her thigh. His fingertips barely brushed the sensitive inside flesh, but he could already feel her responding. Her hands moved across his shoulders, massaging and molding.

Heat merged with pressure in his groin when she made brief, shy contact with his belt buckle. She explored the contours of his sex through his slacks. He found the silky edge of her panties and worked his fingers inside.

He lost all control then, guided by his incredible passion for her. He lifted his head and kissed her fiercely. His hand lingered at the waistband of her panties as he lay beside her on the bed. He teased her through the flimsy fabric for several minutes, reveling in the response it inspired. Sam thrust her body toward him, all the while matching his demanding kiss. He could smell the faint scent of her perfume.

Chase lifted his head again, watching her face as it reddened.

"You're embarrassing me," she said hoarsely.

He liked the husky, sexy tone of her voice and smiled down at her. "I don't think you have a thing to be embarrassed about."

"Why are you staring at me?"

"I'm not staring, sweetheart. I'm admiring," he said just before lowering his mouth to capture one rosy nipple in his mouth. She responded instantly. Sam's fingers played through his hair as he lovingly taunted each rounded peak in turn. Every now and again he would hear a moan from her, and he would respond by placing a kiss on her partially opened mouth.

When he could no longer stand the pressure at his groin, Chase removed her skirt, then his own clothing. He pushed her back against the pillow, using his knee to wedge himself between her legs. He remained balanced above her, watching the expression on her face when his hips met hers. There was still the barrier of their underclothes, but he needed her reassurance.

"I want to make love to you, Sam."

"I want that, too. Very much."

He moved only long enough to remove the last hindrance of their clothing. He could tell almost immediately that she was as ready as he was. Chase had to school himself to move slowly. She wasn't helping him at all as she continued to grind her slender body against his.

"Slow down, Sam, or this won't last more than about ten seconds," he coaxed.

His mouth covered hers before she could speak, though he had a hunch she was beyond the point of lucid conversation. Carefully, he entered her, listening—even expecting some sort of protest. Instead, he heard only words of pleasure, whispered on a warm breath against his mouth.

With a single thrust, he reveled at being deep inside such sweet softness. When she wound her legs around him, Chase groaned and fervently kissed her neck and shoulders before returning to the warm, pliant recesses of her mouth. The rhythm of their lovemaking increased as his hands reached beneath her hips, bringing her even closer to him.

She turned her face away from his, breaking their kiss. "Something's happening to me," she told him, her eyes wide, her pupils dilated with passion.

"Go with it, sweetheart. Trust me, you'll like what happens next."

As predicted, he felt her body convulse with wave after pleasurable wave. The sensation of having her body grip him brought Chase to a fast and furious release.

Apparently afraid of crushing her with his weight, he rolled off her, leaving Sam to wonder at the incredible things her body had just experienced. She was also somewhat surprised that she was no longer concerned about her nakedness. Turning her head, she smiled at her lover. He returned the gesture.

"That was wonderful," she told him. Sam turned in his arms and placed a kiss on his chest. Her fingers toyed with his medallion as she listened to his breathing as it slowly returned to normal.

"WERE YOU on the phone while I was in the shower?" she asked a little later on.

"Why would you think that?"

"You know," Sam said as she rose on tiptoe to place a kiss on his lips, "you have a lot in common with Dr. Masters."

She noted his confused expression. "Me?"

"Yes. The two of you have this thing about answering questions with questions."

Chase's only response was a sexy half smile.

"Ready?"

"Sam—" he placed his hands on her arms "—I don't think this is such a hot idea."

Tilting her head to one side, she regarded his strained expression. Her feelings doubled at the concern she read in his eyes. "I phoned him, and he's not home, so what harm can going over there possibly do?"

"You're not just going over there... You're talking about breaking into a man's apartment. A man who apparently played a hand in getting you out on the night you were attacked."

"I know," she countered. "And after I have a look around, I'll call Detective Burns."

"If you won't let the police handle it, why not let me do it for you?"

Shaking her head, Sam grabbed her purse and pulled him toward the door. "Even if Charlie comes back, he won't hurt me."

"Did this come to you in a vision?"

"No." Sam slapped in the vicinity of his midsection. "Charlie had scads of opportunities to hurt me in the past. It doesn't make sense that he would all of a sudden turn into a crazed killer."

"You didn't have the tape before."

Chase repeated his misgivings as they sat together in the back seat of the cab. Sam wasn't budging—not when she knew she was getting close. She wanted to know Charlie's part in all this. She also needed to know the extent of Karen's complicity. The thought that her friend had betrayed her with silence was heartbreaking for Sam.

The building was a trendy brownstone divided into three apartments. Sam smoothed the front of her black slacks as they crept up the stairs under cover of darkness.

"Stay behind me," he commanded.

She couldn't see around his broad shoulders, but Sam could hear the unmistakable sound of him jiggling the front-door lock. In what seemed like a fraction of a second, Chase had them inside.

"Third floor," she whispered.

The scents of various foods and the low hum of music filtered into the hallways as they made their way up to the top floor. Sam felt her pulse at her temples and knew her heart was racing a mile a minute. Still, she concentrated on moving as soundlessly as possible with her eyes and ears wide open.

Again, Chase did something to the lock on Charlie's apartment which she couldn't see. Whatever the trick, they were inside without ever drawing attention to themselves. It was a good thing, too. Sam was sure she heard someone on the stairs as they eased the door closed.

The apartment was pitch-black and smelled of Charlie's cologne.

"Damn!" she heard Chase call in a whisper a fraction of a second after her ears picked up a dull thudding sound.

Reaching along the wall, Sam found a switch and pressed.

"Oh my Lord," she gasped, her hand flew to her open mouth.

Chase was half sprawled on top of the overturned coffee table. Not an inch of the room had been spared the destruction. Cushions, papers, furniture, knick-knacks—all tossed about or broken.

"I guess Newsome wasn't one to pick up after himself," Chase said as he stood in the center of the pile.

"Who would do this?" Sam whispered.

"Probably someone looking for the tape, I would suspect."

She felt a chill touch each of her vertebrae as it inched up her spine. "I wonder where Charlie is?" she said. Her eyes turned in the direction of a closed door.

"You stay here," Chase told her.

His instruction was easy enough to follow, since Sam was too stunned to move. What if Charlie was dead? What if they'd stumbled onto a murder scene just because she had insisted on undertaking her own investigation?

It was like watching a decoy at a shooting range. Chase weaved through the room, shielding himself whenever possible as he approached the ominous closed door. When Chase reached the door, he grasped the knob in his hand. In one fluid motion, he opened the door and rolled to the opposite side of the jamb.

Nothing.

Crouching, he eased his way into the blackness, his form barely visible to Sam. When she lost sight of him, panic filled the pit of her stomach. Time passed at a crawl.

"Chase?" she whispered.

Nothing.

Sam was about to call out again when her mind registered the fact that the door behind her was opening. Expecting to confront Charlie, Sam whirled in the direction of the sound.

Unless her former agent had grown several inches, the silhouette could not have been his.

"Chase!" she yelled. Then she saw the knife.

One steely hand clamped on her arm, snatching her from the room before the echo of her call for help had faded.

"Don't make a sound," he whispered seethingly into her ear.

The man half carried, half pushed her down the stairs. There was a clattering above them on the stairs, and she felt certain it was Chase. She was torn between wanting him to come to her rescue and the horrible reality that his doing so could prove foolhardy and dangerous.

The knife blade was pressing into the flesh at the base of her throat. He had twisted her arm so that it was wedged painfully behind her back. There was no way she could get away without the likely result being her own demise. Tears filled her eyes as he tugged her down the deserted sidewalk. Not five feet away, there was a steady stream of cars. Sam prayed one of the motorists would see her predicament and summon the police.

His pace was almost too much for her. Fearful of stumbling onto the sharp blade, Sam struggled to keep up. He pulled her into an alleyway, and she immediately felt her throat constrict with the almost certain knowledge that this was going to be it.

She had a vision of Chase's face. At least it *was* a vision until she heard his voice.

"Put it down!" he barked at her captor.

The man stopped and yanked her in front of him. Chase was at the entrance of the alley, no more than four feet away. In his hand, he held a small but lethal-looking revolver.

"I don't think so," the man said coldly.

Sam felt the blade pierce her skin, and she made a small noise.

"I do," Chase said calmly.

Sam heard a popping sound and felt the man holding her tense up before he crumpled backward, pulling her along with him. She had barely fallen when she felt Chase's hands reach around her waist.

"Are you okay? Did he cut you?"

Unable to find her voice, Sam shook her head and buried herself against him. Chase was warm and she felt safe in his embrace.

He felt relief like he had never known before as her warm tears moistened the front of his shirt. Adrenaline still pumped through his veins, but the knot in his gut no longer stole his breath. He rubbed her back with his free hand as the faint wail of sirens became audible over the chorus of horns and tires screeching. He wasn't willing to let her go—not yet.

The entrance to the alley was instantly blocked by unmarked cars with strobing blue lights on their dashboards. Chase lifted her face to him and kissed her hard on the mouth.

"I love you," he said softly. "Please believe that...no matter what."

Her large eyes still glistened with moisture, but she managed to offer him a smile that should have made him feel on top of the world.

"Lawson!"

He faced the source. "Nice to see you, too, O'Malley."

He heard Sam repeat the name as she pulled out of his arms. He didn't have the nerve to look at her. He was afraid of what he might see.

"What the hell have you done?" O'Malley said as he moved toward the body.

"Just what was necessary."

"That's just great," O'Malley snapped, referring to the corpse that lay before them. "Now we'll probably never know what part that Newsome character played in all this.''

"Why the hell not? Where is he, anyway?'' Chase asked.

"Don't know. We had a tail on him, but they lost him a few days ago. We're pretty sure he skipped town, and I doubt if he's ever coming back.''

Several agents with their guns drawn moved past them. Sam blinked as she took in everything around her. She could just make out the face of the man on the ground. There was a small hole above his left eyebrow. The knife was still in his hand.

Involuntarily, she took a step back and turned away. The crackle of radios filled the air around her. The reality of what was going on finally edged out the shock and residual terror.

"O'Malley,'' she whispered.

A man in a blue suit, starched white shirt and cropped hair responded, "I'm Mike O'Malley.''

She met his eyes. They were as aloof as his stoic expression.

"FBI,'' he added.

"And Chase?'' she asked in a weak voice.

"He works for me.''

Chapter Twelve

"His name was Ralston," O'Malley said as he sat across from her at the long conference table. "He has an interesting history with the criminal justice system."

Chase was in the room, too. He stood away from them with his back to her. His hands were rammed into his pockets. The only movement she could detect was the faint rise of his shoulders with each breath.

"Why was he after me?" Sam asked, wrapping her hands around the lukewarm paper cup.

O'Malley stroked his chin. "That's what we were trying to find out."

"So you decided to dangle me in front of him like a carrot in front of a donkey?"

The man had the decency to cringe. "You have to understand, Miss Parrish. Until three hours ago, we weren't even sure if there was someone after you."

"But you and Chase figured it was worth a shot?"

"It wasn't like that," Chase answered softly. Still, he didn't turn around.

"No, it wasn't," O'Malley confirmed. "And we never would have put you in any real danger."

"What do you call being dragged into an alley at knife point?"

"That was an unfortunate turn of events."

"Yes, it was," she agreed, reaching up to run her finger across the small crust of blood where the blade had grazed her skin. "So now what happens?"

O'Malley laced his short fingers together and rested his hands on the table. "That depends on you."

Sam's eyebrows drew together. "What can I do?"

Chase moved then. It took two long strides for him to reach the opposite side of the table from where she sat motionless, watching him.

"Don't do anything, Sam. It's finished."

"Not quite," O'Malley argued. "We still don't know who hired Ralston. Until we do, I'm not certain you'll be safe."

"Put her in Witness Protection," Chase thundered.

"Absolutely not!" Sam huffed. "I want this over."

O'Malley's blue eyes softened with what she assumed was some modicum of respect. Chase's reaction was a different story.

"It's too dangerous!"

"Won't you be with me?" she asked him quietly.

His eyes grew wide at her question. "Me?"

She nodded slowly, still battling her conflicting emotions. "O'Malley told me you weren't a willing participant in all this. Besides, I can't go back to Gillian alone."

"Sam," he said softly as he tilted his head back in apparent exasperation. "You don't have to go back to Gillian. We can set you up with a new—"

"I don't want a new anything. Whoever is behind this has taken my friends and my memory. I'm not willing to give them my life, as well."

"She has a point, Lawson."

"She had a point stuck at her throat, too."

The pain in his voice was genuine. At least she hoped it was. "Then we'll just have to be more careful," she said, forcing optimism to her tone. "And maybe Charlie will reappear, and this will all be cleared up."

"Not likely," O'Malley grunted. "Traces of blood were found in the bathroom of his apartment."

"What about something to explain the tape?" she prodded.

"You can thank your friend Karen for that," O'Malley stated. "On the day she was killed, she mailed this to us." He opened a manila envelope, extracted the contents and slid them toward her.

"Bank statements?" she queried.

Coming around behind her, Chase leaned forward until she could feel his shoulder brush hers. He moistened his finger and flipped through the pages.

"You were mugged on March fifth, right?"

She nodded. Chase could feel her pale eyes boring into his profile.

"Charlie made a deposit of five grand on March fourth, and another five grand on March sixth."

"I see where you're going with this, Chase, but believe me, Charlie couldn't possibly be involved in my mugging. Remember, Charlie got fifteen percent of my earnings from *Secret Splendor,* and I was earning in the low six figures."

"But Charlie had a cash-flow problem. Here, look for yourself."

"DID YOU KNOW?"

Bunny looked up from her adding machine and met Sam's eyes. The shop had opened an hour earlier, and Chase had reluctantly left her in the care of his mother while he tended to a sick animal. Sam was edgy, but she was comforted by the knowledge that there was an agent parked in the lot, just in case.

"I knew."

Sam nodded, having already guessed as much. "I understand why he did it. He also told me that he only came out of retirement because of the people involved. He couldn't turn his back on his friends."

Bunny's smile didn't quite reach her eyes. "Then you are a very understanding woman. My son should not have deceived you. Not in this way."

"I didn't say I was thrilled about it," she admitted. "But that's the past. And you were the one who told me to look to the future."

Bunny laughed. "I hate it when my words come back to haunt me."

"Can I—"

Sam's voice stilled when the door opened. Relief washed over her when she saw a pleasant-looking, middle-aged woman enter. *I've got to stop jumping at every sound,* she admonished herself silently.

"Morning, Mae Joleen!" Bunny called.

"Morning. And Sam, how nice to see you. I heard you were back."

"Sam," Bunny said, "this is Mae Joleen Pace."

MJP. The diary entry instantly flashed across her mind.

"...just stopped in for a soda. I'm meeting my daughter and my grandson for lunch."

Sam gaped at the woman, her mind furiously working toward comprehension. Fairfield Clinic... married... the dates.

"Mrs. Pace?" Sam gushed.

"Miss Pace," the woman corrected.

"Was your daughter born on December 7, 1957?"

Mae Joleen looked stunned, then a smile curved the corners of her deeply lined mouth. "Why...yes."

"At the Fairfield Clinic?"

She nodded.

"And my grandmother knew?"

"What is it, Sam?" Bunny asked. She came around the counter and placed a chubby hand on Sam's shoulder.

"Please, Miss Pace. Did my grandmother have something to do with the birth of your daughter?"

"She helped me make the arrangements at Fairfield. Back in those days, unwed mothers didn't have a lot of options."

"What *exactly* did she do?" Sam pressed.

Mae Joleen was clearly taken aback by the questions but appeared to be willing to relate the story.

"Your grandmother helped girls like me. She either made arrangements at Fairfield, or she supported the ones who gave their babies up. I heard she even had the name of a doctor over near Midgville who would perform the necessary surgery, if you know what I mean. I believe it was known as the Youngblood home."

"And she kept records," Sam whispered. "The diaries were records. Five decades' worth."

"Is something wrong?" Mae Joleen asked. "I didn't upset you, did I?"

Sam grinned at the woman and then placed a loud kiss on her cheek. "Miss Pace, you've made my day. I still don't know who, but I think I know why."

Chase agreed when she told him at his house later that afternoon.

"I knew Gran counseled, but I didn't know she..."

"There must have been something in the diary Grace brought me. Something that would have embarrassed or frightened someone here in Gillian."

"You said she listed marriages?"

Sam nodded. "Maybe there's a bigamist in town. After Gran died, he or she must have realized I would have access to the diaries. You said Grace was the one who cleaned out Gran's house after her death. She must have seen whatever it was."

"Except," Chase interjected, "Patty couldn't have. She rarely came back here from California. I know she was gone long before Gran died. She couldn't have seen the diaries."

"Then," Sam suggested as she reasoned aloud, "it had to be something we all knew. Maybe Grace told Patty and me, and the killer somehow found out."

Chase was smiling at her. His hands were braced on either side of his body where he leaned against the kitchen counter. His shirt gaped open where he'd hastily dressed after his shower. His ebony hair glistened with moisture. Sam tried to swallow the lump in her throat.

"Are you going to laugh at me?" she asked, hoping to break the tension of the electrified space separating them in the narrow room.

"Definitely not," he assured her. "I'm just impressed with your determination. You're getting pretty good at sidestepping the holes I shoot in your theories."

She blushed at the compliment. "I want this behind me," she said.

"And then what?"

His eyes bored into hers.

"Then I get on with my life."

"Do I get—"

Sam cursed the telephone for interrupting him. In the three days since they had been back from New York, Chase had been quiet. She wanted to believe that the feelings he'd expressed that night in her apartment had been genuine and not part of his job description. Several times she had wanted to broach the subject, but she was just too scared of the minute possibility that he would burst her bubble of hope.

"It's Connie," he said as his hand covered the mouth piece. "Do you want to go to a fund-raiser at J.D.'s tonight? Her firm's springing for the tickets."

She nodded. "Sure."

THE GILLIAN ESTATE was quite a shock to Sam. They parked along the U-shaped driveway which was nearly filled with fifty or so cars situated in angles around the landscaped lawn. The building was a series of never-ending arches and deep terra-cotta tiles. The front door was wood with a mosaic tile inlay that was positively one of the prettiest things Sam had ever seen.

"My mother did it," Chase said with definite pride in his voice. "Most of the art and ceramic pieces in this house were commissioned by J.D. Created by my mother's talented hands."

Sam knew Bunny wasn't the only member of the Lawson family with talented hands.

"I'm so glad you're here!" Mildred greeted, adding a hug for good measure.

"Me, too," Connie added, stepping around the blonde and giving Sam's shoulder a squeeze. Her dark hair was hidden by a flattering white turban.

Connie slipped her arm through Sam's and said a quick hello to Chase. She steered Sam through the house to where the bar and food tables were displayed and illuminated by flickering lanterns. There was a four-man band playing Spanish tunes, and the air was thick with the smell of spicy food and resonated with the sounds of laughter.

Sam noticed Connie's shirt and laughed. Emblazoned across the front were the words, I'm A Party Waiting To Happen.

"The pool is gorgeous!" Sam acknowledged as they weaved toward the bar.

"It ought to be," Connie whispered. "The old man had the black marble imported."

Sam let out a low whistle and looked at her friend. She spotted Chase not far behind them and felt more secure in the strange but elaborate surroundings. Jack sat at the bar, and his face lit up when he saw her.

"Nice to see you again," he said as he took her hand. "I was so sorry to hear about your house."

"Nothing a few hammers and some stucco can't fix," she assured him.

"This is my father, J. D. Gillian," Jack said. "Dad, this is Samantha Parrish. Mildred's friend."

"She's evil," the old man muttered.

Sam was so shocked by his hostile greeting that she could do nothing but watch as the elderly man wandered off.

"I'm sorry," Jack said in a discreetly low tone. "Dad gets confused."

"No harm done," she told him with a bright smile.

"Avoiding me?" Chase said against her ear. "Hi, Jack."

"Chase. Good of you to come."

"Thank Connie," Chase said as he faked a punch to the other man's arm. "Her firm paid for the tickets."

"The things I won't do for friends," Connie intoned, fanning herself with one of the cocktail napkins.

"Speaking of which," Chase said as he placed his hand at the small of her back, "I'll show Sam around, if that's all right with you?"

"Feel free," Jack offered amiably. "Just remember, Chase. We're checking the silver before you leave."

"Right," he said with an exaggerated smile.

"What do you want to show me?" Sam asked as he pulled her past the atrium toward the back of the house.

"This," he said as they entered what appeared to be a study. Chase's mouth found hers.

Samantha's heart began to pound, and she turned away from his kiss. His dark eyes never left her face.

"Can you really forgive me for everything that's happened?" They stared at each other in silence. Chase looked so expectant—as if his next breath depended on her answer.

"You don't need my forgiveness," she told him.

"Sam, this afternoon in the kitchen, it was the first time in days you didn't have that pained look in your eyes. It was killing me to think about how much I had hurt you. Believe me, Sam, that was never my intention."

Her mind whirled with dozens of questions, but she knew there was really only one that needed an answer. "That night in my apartment," she began.

"Was real," he finished.

He pulled her to him fiercely, crushing her mouth with his. Sam responded eagerly, molding her soft contours against him. Chase cupped her face in his hands, easing his fingertips into the silken strands of her hair. She tasted so sweet. So sensual. He wished he could lock the door. Take this time to show her how very much she meant to him.

Her hands slipped around his back, tracing his spine with her nails. Her palms pressed against his muscles, applying an urgent pressure that only increased his ardor. She moved against him urgently as she matched the fervor and intensity of his kiss.

He murmured something against her mouth. Something in his native language.

"Thank you."

He lifted his head and smiled at her. "Did you understand what I said?"

"No," she admitted in a sultry voice.

"I said I love you."

She captured her lower lip with her teeth. Her gray eyes fluttered open, still hooded with the remnants of her fiery passion.

"I love you, too."

He kissed her lips, her eyes, the tip of her nose. He nuzzled her neck and drank in the scent of her perfume. He wanted time to stand still. He would gladly spend eternity kissing her, holding her.

"We have to get back," she said against his ear.

"I know," he agreed, though his lips lingered just above the hollow of her throat.

"We *really* have to get back," she said as her hands gently pushed him away.

"Mildred would die if she knew we were rolling around in the old man's study," he said wryly.

Her cheeks grew warm as she ducked out of his arms and straightened her blouse. "We didn't roll."

"But we could," he suggested with an outrageous wink.

"No. Especially not in here. J.D. already thinks I'm evil."

"What are you talking about?" he asked.

She told him about the bizarre comment at the bar. "I wonder why he doesn't like me," she said as they walked down the hall hand in hand.

"He's not all there, Sam. Don't take it to heart."

"I won't."

"There you two are!" Connie pounced on them as they neared the glass doors. "Tsk, tsk. You two look like a couple of guilty teenagers. What were you doing, Chase? Showing her the etchings?"

"Very funny," he told her. Chase placed his free arm across Connie's shoulders. "No date?"

"Tyler went back to Montana," she said with a sigh. "Your brother Cody's married. You're apparently taken. I guess that leaves the members of the band." Connie's eyebrows lifted in an exaggerated arch. "Let me see, there're four of them . . ."

"That sounds about right," Chase said with a nod.

"I almost forgot," Connie said as they moved out onto the veranda, "there was a call for you, Chase. Somebody named O'Malley."

"Keep an eye on Sam for me, will you?"

He brushed the top of Sam's head with a kiss before slipping back into the house.

"The two of you seem quite chummy," Connie observed.

Sam met the woman's dark eyes and knew instantly that it would be impossible to hide her feelings. "Things are . . . nice."

"Dresses are nice," Connie explained as they strolled toward the pool. "Men are exciting."

"Then things are definitely exciting."

"Mildred will eat this up. She has always believed in love and marriage."

"How about you?" Sam asked.

Connie grabbed a small sandwich off a tray and nibbled the edge. "I'm not ready for all that stuff yet. I'm not very good at commitment."

"But you have your own real-estate firm. Isn't that a commitment?"

Connie smiled. "I've seen so many people destroy themselves in the name of love. I guess I'm just gun-shy."

Sam wanted to tell her that it wasn't like that. It was a warm, wonderful feeling that made your heart burst with joy. She wanted to, but she didn't have the chance. Connie was whisked away by some man insisting that they discuss some sort of lease.

Sam looked around at the expertly landscaped grounds. She was well within earshot of the hundred or so people milling around the lawn. Chase was nearby, and so she allowed herself to relax and bask in the glowing memories of his kiss. Absently, her fingers went to her lips. If she closed her eyes, she imagined she could still feel the urgent pressure of his mouth on hers.

"This way, Sam," a female voice hissed from the shadows.

"I'VE GOT to go!" Chase barked into the receiver.

"Is she with you? Can you see her?"

"No! I'll call you back."

Chase sprinted from the house, very nearly toppling J.D. in his hasty exit. "Sorry," he mumbled as he steadied the frail man.

"She's down by the pool."

He looked questioningly at J.D.

"The evil one," he explained.

He reached into his boot and retrieved his revolver from its holster as he moved stealthily toward the poolside cabana. He pulled up short at the door and listened for any sound.

"You have been a real problem, Sam."

"Mildred, don't do this," she appealed. "You won't get away with it."

Mildred's green eyes grew wide and wild. "I don't have a choice. If any of it gets out, it will cost Jack the election."

"*It* what?" Sam schooled her voice to sound calm, praying it might buy her some time.

Mildred snorted and the gun in her hand shook slightly. "I had an abortion in high school. Your grandmother told me I would regret it. I do, but not for the reasons she spelled out."

"Lots of people have abortions," Sam countered.

"But they aren't engaged to a senator who has built a career on the importance of preserving the family."

"But surely you and he can—"

"Jack doesn't know!" Mildred snapped. "No one knew but the four of us. I couldn't risk one of you making it public."

"But we were all friends," Sam implored. She had to keep Mildred talking—talking was definitely much better than shooting. She glanced around, hoping to find something that she could use as a weapon.

That was when she saw Chase.

Soundlessly, he moved into the room behind Mildred. Tucking the gun into his waistband, he reached for the swimmers' hook resting against the floor. The hum of the filter drowned out the sound as he swung it through the air, hooking the surprised Mildred and tossing her to the ground. Unfortunately, her gun discharged.

"Sam!" he screamed.

"I'm fine!" she responded.

Chase pounced on the flailing woman. Ripping the gun from her hand, he sent it skittering across the uneven concrete floor. Unarmed, Mildred stilled beneath him. The woman stared up at him with chilling, evil eyes, brimming with hatred.

Epilogue

The chapel was decorated in a fragrant array of flowers. Clutching her stomach, Sam looked at the clock
on the wall only to find that less than three minutes
had passed.

"You still have time to back out," Connie quipped.

Sam smiled at her maid of honor.

"Don't give her any ideas," Caitlin chided.

Sam's soon-to-be sister-in-law was standing in front
of a mirror, positioning her bouquet over her very
pregnant abdomen. Bunny stood behind Caitlin,
fussing with the train of the bridesmaid's gown that
had needed constant refitting.

"I don't want to back out," Sam assured them. "I
just want it to start!"

The first note of the processional vibrated through
the small room.

"That is my cue," Bunny said. Moving to Sam, she
bent forward, kissed her cheek, then wiped away the

smudge of lipstick. "Here," she whispered and placed a small box in Sam's hand before leaving the room.

"How beautiful!" Sam exclaimed as she lifted the hinged top. Inside, she found a small silver medallion that was a perfect miniature of the one Chase always wore.

"Lawson tradition," Caitlin explained.

There was a series of gentle taps on the door.

"That's us," Connie announced.

"Fasten this around my neck for me," Sam asked her friend as she handed her flowers to Caitlin.

"What about the other chain?"

Sam thought about the key Karen had given her all those months ago. "Take it off," she instructed.

Connie obliged her by replacing the old with the new.

"How do I look?" Sam asked when the tapping on the door resumed.

"You look like a bride," Connie assured her. "Make that a nervous bride."

Connie's assessment had been right. Sam was so nervous that she barely remembered the service or the reception. All she remembered was the way Chase's eyes had conveyed his love as they had exchanged their vows.

"You're smiling," he said as he popped the cork on the champagne bottle at the hotel that night.

"I'm very happy."

The ring on his left hand reflected the flame from the candle in the center of their suite. "I'm glad you're happy, Sam."

"How glad?" she teased, inching closer so that she was all but in his lap.

"You want me to show you?"

"Uh-huh," she murmured against his throat.

Chase drew her to him swiftly, holding her at an angle so that his long fingers could work on the buttons of her blouse. "Did you wear this complicated thing on purpose?"

Sam giggled. "It was Connie's suggestion. She said it would teach you to be a patient husband."

"She was wrong," he said as he peeled back the layer of her clothing. "God, you're beautiful."

Sam inhaled the heady scent of his cologne. She loved everything about him. The warmth of his skin, the softness of his straight black hair. Her hands found his chest, and she brazenly began to massage the taut muscles beneath her palms.

He moaned when he released the front clasp of her bra, then moved his mouth to her body. He teased, taunted and inspired. There was something so intense and yet so gentle about the ways he made love to her. It was tender and yet all-consuming. She knew there was nothing else that could compare to the feeling of being in his arms.

"What's this?" he asked, lifting his head and rubbing the pad of his thumb over her necklace where the silver medallion dangled in the valley between her breasts.

"Your mother gave it to me."

"What about the key?"

"It's in a safe place," she told him as she kissed each of his lips in turn.

"I ... thought ... it ... was ... important."

She caught his head in her hands and looked directly into his eyes. "You're what's important, Chase. Only you."

Where do you find hot Texas nights, smooth Texas charm and dangerously sexy cowboys?

Crystal Creek reverberates with the exciting rhythm of Texas.
Each story features the rugged individuals who live and love in the
Lone Star State.

"...Crystal Creek wonderfully evokes the hot days and steamy nights of
a small Texas community...impossible to put down until the last page
is turned."
—*Romantic Times*

"...a series that should hook any romance reader. Outstanding."
—*Rendezvous*

Praise for Margot Dalton's *Even the Nights Are Better*

"...every bit as engrossing as the others. Ms. Dalton wraps you in
sentiment...this is a book you don't just read, you feel."
—*Rendezvous*

Don't miss the next book in this exciting series. Look for
SOUTHERN NIGHTS by Margot Dalton

Available in June wherever Harlequin books are sold.

This July,
Harlequin and Silhouette
are proud to bring you

By Request™

CONVENIENTLY Yours

WANTED: Husband
POSITION: Temporary
TERMS: Negotiable—but must be willing to live in.

And falling in love is definitely not part of the
contract!

Relive the romance....

Three complete novels by your favorite authors—in
one special collection!

TO BUY A GROOM by Rita Clay Estrada
MEETING PLACE by Bobby Hutchinson
THE ARRANGEMENT by Sally Bradford

Available wherever
Harlequin and Silhouette books are sold.

HARLEQUIN® **V** *Silhouette*®

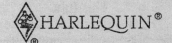

HARLEQUIN®

WEDDING INVITATION
Marisa Carroll

Brent Powell is marrying Jacqui Bertrand, and the whole town of Eternity is in on the plans. This is to be the first wedding orchestrated by the newly formed community co-op, Weddings, Inc., and no detail is being overlooked.

Except perhaps a couple of trivialities. The bride is no longer speaking to the groom, his mother is less than thrilled with her, and her kids want nothing to do with *him.*

WEDDING INVITATION, available in June from Superromance, is the first book in Harlequin's exciting new cross-line series, **WEDDINGS, INC.** Be sure to look for the second book, **EXPECTATIONS,** by Shannon Waverly (Harlequin Romance #3319), coming in July.

WED-1

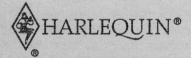

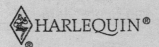

INDULGE A LITTLE 6947 SWEEPSTAKES
NO PURCHASE NECESSARY

HERE'S HOW THE SWEEPSTAKES WORKS:
The Harlequin Reader Service shipments for January, February and March 1994 will contain, respectively, coupons for entry into three prize drawings: a trip for two to San Francisco, an Alaskan cruise for two and a trip for two to Hawaii. To be eligible for any drawing using an Entry Coupon, simply complete and mail according to directions.

There is no obligation to continue as a Reader Service subscriber to enter and be eligible for any prize drawing. You may also enter any drawing by hand printing your name and address on a 3" x 5" card and the destination of the prize you wish that entry to be considered for (i.e., San Francisco trip, Alaskan cruise or Hawaiian trip). Send your 3" x 5" entries to: Indulge a Little 6947 Sweepstakes, c/o Prize Destination you wish that entry to be considered for, P.O. Box 1315, Buffalo, NY 14269-1315, U.S.A. or Indulge a Little 6947 Sweepstakes, P.O. Box 610, Fort Erie, Ontario L2A 5X3, Canada.

To be eligible for the San Francisco trip, entries must be received by 4/30/94; for the Alaskan cruise, 5/31/94; and the Hawaiian trip, 6/30/94. No responsibility is assumed for lost, late or misdirected mail. Sweepstakes open to residents of the U.S. (except Puerto Rico) and Canada, 18 years of age or older. All applicable laws and regulations apply. Sweepstakes void wherever prohibited.

For a copy of the Official Rules, send a self-addressed, stamped envelope (WA residents need not affix return postage) to: Indulge a Little 6947 Rules, P.O. Box 4631, Blair, NE 68009, U.S.A.

INDR93

INDULGE A LITTLE 6947 SWEEPSTAKES
NO PURCHASE NECESSARY

HERE'S HOW THE SWEEPSTAKES WORKS:
The Harlequin Reader Service shipments for January, February and March 1994 will contain, respectively, coupons for entry into three prize drawings: a trip for two to San Francisco, an Alaskan cruise for two and a trip for two to Hawaii. To be eligible for any drawing using an Entry Coupon, simply complete and mail according to directions.

There is no obligation to continue as a Reader Service subscriber to enter and be eligible for any prize drawing. You may also enter any drawing by hand printing your name and address on a 3" x 5" card and the destination of the prize you wish that entry to be considered for (i.e., San Francisco trip, Alaskan cruise or Hawaiian trip). Send your 3" x 5" entries to: Indulge a Little 6947 Sweepstakes, c/o Prize Destination you wish that entry to be considered for, P.O. Box 1315, Buffalo, NY 14269-1315, U.S.A. or Indulge a Little 6947 Sweepstakes, P.O. Box 610, Fort Erie, Ontario L2A 5X3, Canada.

To be eligible for the San Francisco trip, entries must be received by 4/30/94; for the Alaskan cruise, 5/31/94; and the Hawaiian trip, 6/30/94. No responsibility is assumed for lost, late or misdirected mail. Sweepstakes open to residents of the U.S. (except Puerto Rico) and Canada, 18 years of age or older. All applicable laws and regulations apply. Sweepstakes void wherever prohibited.

For a copy of the Official Rules, send a self-addressed, stamped envelope (WA residents need not affix return postage) to: Indulge a Little 6947 Rules, P.O. Box 4631, Blair, NE 68009, U.S.A.

INDR93

INDULGE A LITTLE
SWEEPSTAKES

OFFICIAL ENTRY COUPON

This entry must be received by: JUNE 30, 1994
This month's winner will be notified by: JULY 15, 1994
Trip must be taken between: AUGUST 31, 1994-AUGUST 31, 1995

YES, I want to win the 3-Island Hawaiian vacation for two. I understand that the prize includes round-trip airfare, first-class hotels and pocket money as revealed on the "wallet" scratch-off card.

Name_____

Address _____ Apt. _____

City_____

State/Prov._____ Zip/Postal Code_____

Daytime phone number_____
                              (Area Code)

Account #_____

Return entries with invoice in envelope provided. Each book in this shipment has two entry coupons—and the more coupons you enter, the better your chances of winning!
© 1993 HARLEQUIN ENTERPRISES LTD.   MONTH3

INDULGE A LITTLE
SWEEPSTAKES

OFFICIAL ENTRY COUPON

This entry must be received by: JUNE 30, 1994
This month's winner will be notified by: JULY 15, 1994
Trip must be taken between: AUGUST 31, 1994-AUGUST 31, 1995

YES, I want to win the 3-Island Hawaiian vacation for two. I understand that the prize includes round-trip airfare, first-class hotels and pocket money as revealed on the "wallet" scratch-off card.

Name_____

Address _____ Apt. _____

City_____

State/Prov._____ Zip/Postal Code_____

Daytime phone number_____
                              (Area Code)

Account #_____

Return entries with invoice in envelope provided. Each book in this shipment has two entry coupons—and the more coupons you enter, the better your chances of winning!
© 1993 HARLEQUIN ENTERPRISES LTD.   MONTH3